Now You Don't

ISBN: 9781072944096

This is a work of fiction. Names, characters, businesses, places, events, groups, and incidents are either the products the author's imagination or used in a fictitious manner. Any resemblance to actual persons, living or dead, or actual events is purely coincidental.

Edits by: Tory Hunter
Cover art: Megan Ransdell

For Dad, Willie, and Taylor

Chapter 1

To experience pain for the first time is to experience life at its fullest.

Only the strong were able to inhale the adrenaline-inducing, euphoric wave that rolled through them as they struck back at their immediate danger. The disgraces, the ones who ran away and hid, were killed and forgotten. Who would want to remember a coward when you could remember the bravest of the brave, the hero, the one who knew that pain, in all its glory, was only temporary and dragged on as long as one lets it?

That was why *he* didn't let it drag on for that long. Instead, he set out to conquer, which is why no one messed with him anymore. It had been days since anyone had approached, in fact. Not that he could blame them. The last king that came to try and take his land was slaughtered on the spot by an unnamed hero and mercenary hired by, well, one could say the king of this land.

Yes, that's right. *He* was ready to protect his land and people at any cost necessary. He was the king, after all. Strong, strikingly handsome, and not to mention intelligent. He had a plan for everything. Whether he had to use brute force, seduction, or strategy. No longer did he or his people have to fear anything. He was the savior of the land of rolling green hills, giant trolls, and defenseless, peaceful wood elves. There was no need for any of them to thank him, though. He did this for the joy of bringing justice to a land of chaos and a land that no longer knew-

"You… wanted to speak with someone?"

His eyes lifted from the game on his phone to the bright, wooden walls around him. He scanned them with haste, taking in the elegant woodwork lining the top and bottom. Right above the sign labeled 'Captain's Quarters' was a symbol carved deep into the wood. A swirl in the middle, coming off to one tail, a branch coming off that tail, and three more branches coming off that one.

His eyes went back down to the rather large man who was giving him a quizzical stare. With the attire he wore – dirtied up blue jeans, a black, long-sleeved shirt, and apron – he looked like one of the *workers* around here. Maybe a cook of some sort?

"Yes, the owner of this ship."

"I'm afraid he's not here. Can I be any help?" the large man asked.

"No, I really don't think you can. When will he be back?"

The man was sweaty, like he was nervous about something. His eyes shifted slightly every three seconds or so, his fingers did dances on his pant legs, and his lip… it twitched just enough to be noticeable. He was trying to hide it, though, which he was good at. To the untrained eye, he would look like a normal person.

"Well, we're about four days in," the man said. "So three days. Probably."

"Probably?"

"He's handling personal business."

His fingers were squirming faster now. He was getting irritated, it seemed. He was uncomfortable with this *personal* business.

"I understand."

"Are you sure there's nothing I can do to help, Mister...?" The man paused.

"Oh, my apologizes. My name's not important. I'm just an acquaintance of Eric's."

He stood and reached out to shake the man's hand before flashing a smile.

"Should I let him know you were-"

"I'll see him before you will. And if not, he'll know I was here."

He turned, leaving the man standing speechless, staring at the back of his head. He wasn't sure what this man knew, so saying his name could possibly be problematic. It'd cause an uproar, chaos... stuff he didn't have time for.

Besides, he was on a cruise. If he had to wait out the rest of the days until they got to Massachusetts, he might as well enjoy himself.

He closed the door behind him and headed down the long hallway towards his room. He'd ordered room service, his stomach reminded him, and he couldn't wait to dig into his BLT. It'd been forever since he'd had meat, and he couldn't understand how anyone could go their entire lives without it.

"Levi!"

Levi spun around at the sound of his name. The tone was low pitched and unfamiliar, almost like that of the worker he was talking to-

"What-" Levi's voice cut off with a sigh. "Dammit, Kara. You've got to stop doing that to me."

Kara shrugged her way around the plant she was hiding behind with a goofy grin on her face. Except, it wasn't her *normal* face. She'd transformed her outer appearance into that of a man's, which was also why her voice was deeper.

"Well, when you stop falling for it, maybe I will," she said, and her features melded back into their usual soft, feminine self. "So, is he here? You're still in one piece, but you're a little jumpier than usual."

"He's off on some 'personal' business," Levi said. "Meaning Cerva was right. It's already beginning."

Kara brushed her blonde hair behind her shoulders, revealing the dark green mark on her neck. The small swirl started at the base and curved its way up below her ear, coming to a leaf-shaped circle at the end.

"Hey, hey." Levi pulled her hair back over top of it. "We're going to have to be more careful while we're here. These people – the workers know what Eric's looking for, and yours is awful close."

She slapped his hand out of the way.

"I don't need to hide mine. It looks like a tattoo," she growled. "Besides. If any of these guys know anything about these marks, they know not to target me."

Kara was from the Silvan tribe… meaning she was basically a forest person. She could use healing magic that originated from the earth, and she could also cast some elemental magic, but mostly just the earth magic. Other tribes didn't target the Silvan because they were important to the balance of nature. However, occasionally you'd hear about someone from the Lupus or Vulpes tribe getting a little too ambitious.

"Well, they don't. None of these guys belong to a specific tribe," Levi said. "They all seem to be some kind of mix. I haven't seen a trace of a mark on any of them."

"Wait, hold on." Kara wrinkled her nose. "If Eric isn't here, why are all these guys still working? They're prisoners. Shouldn't they be trying to make a run for it?"

"You'd think."

Kara shook her head.

"So what now?" she asked. "We have less than a week."

"Well, we can't do anything right now." Levi shrugged. "Might as well enjoy ourselves while we have the chance, yeah?"

He knew Kara was glaring at him, but he didn't know why. They couldn't very well swim to shore or anything. He didn't even know where they were relative to where they needed to be.

"Fine," Kara said. "By the way, that BLT you ordered was delicious."

"What?" Levi asked, but Kara turned towards their room. "Hey? My sandwich?"

Chapter 2

"Thank god," Kara said. "I thought we'd never make it."

Levi scanned the area, his attention settling on the dock where several of the workers were unloading cargo from the ship. They appeared to be just like everyone, trying to earn a living in this dull, gloomy city, but to Levi, they stood out like a sore thumb. He'd never been to Massachusetts before, but he'd been to America. This place looked the same as everywhere else did. People shoulder to shoulder, staring down at their phones, and not paying attention to anything around them. But the workers…they flinched during any interaction whatsoever. They didn't even gaze in awe at the skyscrapers, small patches of vegetation, and the quiet congregations of people socializing and having a good time.

"So, where do you think he-"

"This isn't the place," Levi said, shrugging past people. "The buildings don't look the same."

"How do you figure?"

Everywhere in America might look the same, but the place that Cerva showed him was the one exception. The buildings were huge, the sidewalk and streets even more crowded… where was this place?

"Hey," Levi said, his eyes zeroing in on a spot on the sidewalk. "Be right back. I'm going to check this out."

Below him, every stone of the sidewalk was in perfect order. None of them were off center, chipped, or anything. None except – he reached out and wrapped his hand around the one stone sticking straight up in the air. It was firm. There didn't seem to be any give in its structure or the stones around it. It was as if someone had reached down and scooped it up from the foundation without any trouble.

"Levi? What is it?"

Levi chuckled as he pulled his pocket watch from his tan overcoat.

"Magic," he said, glancing down to see that the time and date were different than before. "Let's see what we can figure out."

Everyone around him slowed to a stop, and as soon as Levi clicked the top button on his watch, they started walking backwards. At first it was in slow motion, but soon enough people, lighting, and animals flew past him. It turned night, then day, then back and forth until –

"How do you know what day to go back to?" Kara asked.

"It does it on its own," Levi said. "It picks up the traces of magic left behind and dates it."

Using the pocket watch he *borrowed* from the Mus tribe meant that he could, in a sense, travel back in time. He wasn't physically there. He could just see the events that unfolded on any given time and day. And as long as Kara knew he was doing it, she could use her magic to come and see, too.

"Look, Levi, the stone's back in-"

"Stop standing there like a buffoon."

Nostalgia rushed Levi as he turned his head. His body froze up, and he nearly dropped the pocket watch as his hands fell to his sides. His lips parted as he tried to say something, anything, really, but the air around him was gone.

The scrawny, black-haired boy in front of him glared in the direction of the man who'd shoved him out of the way, glanced around to make sure no one was watching, and whispered something under his breath.

That was when the stone popped up, sending the man to the ground. Levi's eyes went back to the boy, who tried unsuccessfully to stifle the giggle from his lips.

"I…" Levi struggled to say. "O-Ollie…"

"Hey," the man said, dusting off his blue buttoned up shirt. "Did you do that, kid?"

Oliver looked stunned as he shook his head, but the man continued to stare at him.

"No, honest."

His voice was still the same as it used to be: quiet and guilty. It was the same one he'd used whenever they got in trouble with their parents for whatever they did at the time. The thought made Levi almost smile.

But this magic he was using. He was barely able to use any the last time they saw each other, and, to Levi's understanding, none of the workers on the ship were allowed to use magic. So he couldn't have been practicing.

"Then what's so funny about me falling?"

Again, Oliver shook his head, backing up as the man neared him.

How had he grown up so much? It'd been years since he'd seen his little brother, but it felt more like a lifetime. Everything about him was different. His voice was deep instead of the shrill, high-pitched tone he remembered. His face had filled out and now shared their mother's soft, gentle features. It was like Levi was looking at someone he didn't even know.

"Nothing, sir," Oliver said, his back against a wall. "I wasn't laughing."

"I think you were," the man said, now right in his face. "Do you want to make a problem?"

"Um, no, I-"

Oliver's eyes widened as the man's right hand rose and came towards him open-palmed.

"Dammit," Levi said. "I swear-"

Oliver's eyes widened and an apple from the table to his right went flying, hitting the man in the hand.

"I didn't know your brother was good with his magic," Kara whispered, as if someone might hear her.

Levi shook his head.

"Did… did you do that, too?" the man asked, his face a dark shade of red when he looked back up.

Oliver was speechless as his eyes cycled from the apple to the man.

A hand wrapped around Oliver's shirt as he was lifted from the ground and slammed up against the wall.

"Oh my god," Levi groaned. "He's going to get himself clobbered."

"You're going to regret-"

"Hey! Hey! You put him down right now."

Levi's head whipped around to see a young, blue-haired girl standing directly behind him. She was barely shorter than he was, filled out but not necessarily overweight. It was more muscle than extra padding. Her brown eyes glared a hole through the man's head and even made Levi shiver and back out of her way.

"Do you know him?" the man asked.

"No, but I'm not going to let you pick on some kid." Her voice was daring, and as he hesitated to drop Oliver, her jaw clenched. "Put him down and get outta here. Mind your business."

Oliver's feet hit the ground as the man snorted and backed away. He eyed the girl up and down and slowly made his way back in the same direction as before, over the stone sticking up in the middle of the path.

"I don't believe this," Levi said. "Cerva was right. Ollie's magic is getting stronger."

"But the seal your mother put on him," Kara said. "Shouldn't that keep it at bay?"

"It should."

This didn't make any sense at all. His mother was the strongest Cerva to have ever lived, meaning her sealing magic was like none other. There was no way he was able to break through such mastery.

But the magic Oliver had used in the vision Cerva sent to him…

Eric barely pulled back fast enough as the beam of fire exploded from Oliver's hand.

That was the kind of magic only someone with uncapped power could use. Meaning that Oliver's mark really had broken through the seal. Not that he needed any other proof. The new tail coming off his mark and burning on his lower back was evidence enough.

"Hey, come on," Kara said, turning Levi around. "They're getting away."

The two of them followed Oliver and this girl, listening to them go through introductions and talk about the cruise ship. But Levi barely heard a word of it. He couldn't stop staring at his little, but not so much anymore, brother.

A twinge of guilt stabbed his stomach. He couldn't believe he'd missed out on watching Oliver grow up. Not that it was entirely his fault. Their father...

He shook his head. He didn't have time to reminisce. He needed to find out where Oliver had run off to.

"Well," Oliver whispered. "I-I have magic."

Levi felt like he'd been gut punched as his mouth dropped open. His eyes moved to Kara, who was staring at Oliver with a look of disbelief.

That was... so stupid. Why would he say something like that after being told his entire life to hide from the world?

Did Oliver not remember the countless lectures and yelling fights Levi and their dad had over telling someone about their magic?

Levi's eyes went to their father's as he stormed into the room, his eyes wild. At first, Levi wasn't sure who he was headed for, since Levi was the one holding the car battery, but Oliver was the one who had nearly sparked it to life with his magic. Had their father been spying on them somehow?

"What's going on in here?" Their dad's voice was rugged.

"Dad, please. I was just showing him-"

Levi's eyes widened as their dad headed for Oliver.

"Oliver, what did we tell you about using your magic?" their dad seethed.

"B-But, I-"

Levi's hand caught their dad's wrist before he could touch Oliver. Their eyes met, and for a second, Levi didn't recognize their father's slate-colored eyes glaring back at him.

"If you ever lay finger on him, I swear that you'll regret it," Levi said.

"Get out of my house, you ungrateful-"

"What did he just say?" Levi asked nervously.

The girl stopped, her face not surprised one bit. In fact, she almost seemed unimpressed.

"So, you're a magician?" she asked, and both Kara's and Levi's heads whipped to Oliver.

"A-A magician?" Oliver laughed, but she just stared at him. "Oh, you're serious. Um, yeah, I guess. A magician."

"Well, if you want, you can perform in the lobby or something," she said. "I'm sure dad would be okay with that."

The image around them slowly began to warp as Levi's thumb pushed the button on his pocket watch. Before they could even blink, they were back where they started, standing by the only askew stone on the entire stretch of sidewalk.

"So, then…where is he?" Kara asked.

"There's a hotel up just ahead of where we were at," Levi said. "I bet it's that one."

Unfortunately, the Mus tribe's magic wasn't advanced enough for their pocket watch to go forever. If it had enough power, he would've followed them the whole way. But they eventually caught back up to where they were in the 'vision,' and continued, following the map on Levi's phone.

"So what are you going to say to him?" Kara asked. Levi gave her a funny look. "You know, when you see your brother again for the first time."

Levi sighed as he let his neck give way to the weight of his head, and he stared up at the greying sky. There was a lot he wanted to say to Oliver. It felt like they'd been away from one another their entire lives. Should he ask him the basic questions? The ones he *should* know the answers to because they were brothers? He knew more than anything else that he wanted to apologize to Oliver for not being there to stop Eric. Even if he had been there, he would've just gotten killed along with their sister and mom.

"I dunno."

"Well, you haven't seen him in a while."

"Eight years," he said, his head coming back to level. "Eight years…"

It was all because he couldn't keep Oliver in the dark about their family's magic. But maybe it would've been better. If Oliver hadn't found out about his magic, maybe the seal wouldn't have been broken.

"Come on, come on! One more time!" Oliver pleaded. "I can do it. Just show me one more time."

Levi glanced nervously around the room again before he whispered a spell under his breath. Their mom and dad had been out and about all day, but he wasn't sure when they'd be back, or if they already were. If his father knew what he was doing…

"Just like this, yeah?" The flame relit in his hand. "And you don't want to yell your spell. Just a quick mumble'll do."

He knew it didn't matter how you said the spell. Loud, soft, Latin, Spanish, English, it was all the same. You just had to draw your energy in one place and concentrate. However, whispering was the only thing keeping their mom and dad from knowing what they were doing, assuming they were around.

A tiny ball of fire appeared in Oliver's hand. He gasped and looked up at Levi in amazement.

"Look at it!" Oliver said. "I did it!"

"Knew you could." Levi ruffled his brother's hair. "Now let's make sure we don't do this around Mom or Dad, oka-"

Levi froze as he heard the creaking floorboard behind him.

"You-" his dad said. Levi spun around to find him standing in the doorway. "You didn't."

"Dad, I-"

"The curse, Levi!" His father's face was red. "You're in and out of our lives. A failure. Oliver was doing just fine and now you've cursed him!"

Levi shook his head, backing away.

"Dad, he can use magic. You know that," he said. "It was just a little flame."

"We made it disappear for him. You've cursed him."

Honestly, he really didn't think Oliver was going to be able to do it with his mark sealed. They were just messing around.

"Did you hear me?"

"Huh?" Levi shook his head as he realized they were in front of a large building.

Kara glared at him and pulled on the metal doors.

"I said it's locked. All the lights are off, and there aren't any cars in the lot."

Locked? In the middle of the day? That couldn't be right.

Levi stepped forward and pulled on the doors, too, just to make sure. Again, Kara gave him a look of pure agitation.

"Well, this isn't going to do." He kneeled to eye level with the lock. "Gimme a sec."

"Levi!" Kara said. "Right now? What if someone sees us?"

When Levi was younger, he lived with an old married couple in Germany while he attended school. The man, Ernst, was a locksmith, so Levi knew how to take care of locks with ease. He did get in trouble for it a lot with Lina, the woman, who would then scold her husband. But the two of them just laughed about it together later while she was gone.

"What if there's an alarm?" Kara said, but Levi continued to work. "Levi!"

"Relax." The lock popped and the door came open. "The only thing that's going to get us in trouble is you being so loud. If we look like we belong, no one will question it, yeah?"

"Yeah," she mumbled.

They made their way inside, where the smell of bleach and disinfectant spray filled their noses. Whoever owned this place really kept it clean.

Levi pulled out the pocket watch and once again clicked the button. But time didn't rewind for long before he had to stop it because-

"Hello, sir, how can I help you?" A rounded, older man stood behind the desk. His plump cheek rested against his beefy, sausage-like fingers, and his arm leaned on the desk for support. He had a relaxed posture, but he radiated worry. Levi could just tell.

"Have you seen a little boy wandering around the last couple days? Tall, tan, black hair?" A chill ran down Levi's spine as he spun around. Standing behind him was a tall, black man in a neatly pressed suit. Even though Levi knew Eric wasn't able to see him, he still struggled to swallow the lump in his throat. "He might've been a little off. Very polite," the man said.

The round man's face went pale, and Levi could tell that Eric was thinking the same thing. He looked like he was about to faint, but color soon came back to him, and he straightened up.

"Uh, yes! Yes! His name was…" The man hit his head a couple times. "Oliver? Oliver! He ran off with my daughter! Do you know where he is?"

"I don't, but I need you to think," Eric said as he flashed his *charming* smile. "Where would they run off to? This boy has never been to America, so your daughter would be his guide."

The hotel clerk rubbed his temples with his swollen fingers for what felt like forever. Eric was visibly getting impatient. He was on a mission, a hunt. His prey was close but the more time he wasted the further they slipped away.

"Oh, um, New York, maybe? Her mother was from New York and we took her to visit family sometimes," the man said. "She really wanted to go to NYU, too. Maybe she went around that area?"

New York!

That explained the number of people, all the tall buildings, and why Eric and Oliver were on a skyscraper.

"Why don't we go find them, hm?" Eric asked. "I don't know your daughter, and the boy's very easy to lose. Maybe you can help me."

"Yes! Yes, of course! Let me get everyone out of here and I'll be right back." The clerk waddled hastily around the desk. "The name's Mason O'Bannon, by the way."

"Eric Bain. It's a pleasure."

The scene around them stopped, and time rushed forward, back to the present.

"NYU," Kara said. "That means the building you saw had to be an apartment or something around there."

"Then that's where we need to go." Levi tucked the watch back into his pocket.

Oliver was just days away from jumping off the edge of a building for… well, Levi didn't know why. Maybe his little brother had discovered the trick that would end Eric's hunt. Something their mother tried to do years before she died. Levi had considered doing the same while he was in Russia, but Kara wouldn't let him. She said that with the seal around Oliver's mark, Eric would never know he was one of the last two Cerva.

But here they were. And it was all Levi's fault. If he hadn't shown Oliver his magic, Oliver would be safe.

A little unhappy, maybe, but anything was better than *dead.*

Chapter 3

"We're taking a *taxi* from Massachusetts to New York?" Kara asked as Levi hung up his phone.

"Well, I could drive, but I don't have a license if we get pulled over," Levi said. "And I'm brown and you're Russian, so you know how that'll go."

Kara rolled her eyes as the taxi pulled up, and Levi opened her door.

"We going to NYU, right?" the driver asked. Levi nodded.

"Alright."

As the driver pulled onto the interstate, Levi leaned back in his seat and stared out the window. He wondered how Oliver was able to make it so far around here. He'd been kind of helpless and sheltered when they were younger, so Levi couldn't imagine his little brother doing anything out of his comfort zone. It must be that girl with him.

Lynn.

She was making him brave.

The thought made him chuckle. He was the same way when he first left home. Helpless and naïve. He wised up quickly, though, while he was in Russia, also with the help of a daring, hard-headed girl.

"Wait," Kara whispered. "If you were driving and we did get caught, you could just use your mental magic. Problem solved."

"I could." Levi scratched his neck. "But I'm not supposed to. Cerva doesn't like it."

"Since when do you take orders from someone?"

Levi sighed as he gazed out the window at the passing scenery. There weren't a lot of trees or open fields like he was used to seeing. In fact, with each passing second, he realized just how overindustrialized everything was.

"She's a goddess, yeah? I always do what she says."

"You hardly ever obey Cerva," Kara said. "In fact, she complains to Silva all the time that you-"

"Alright, alright. I just didn't wanna drive, okay?" Levi interrupted. "There. Happy? Besides, we've got a couple days before Ollie skydives."

Plus, he needed time to figure out what the hell he was going to do once he got there. Saving his brother was one thing, but what about after that? Eric would be right on top of them, and it'd be a tight squeeze to get away. But it was just the three of them. Surely there was some way they could slip out undetected. Hopefully.

"Levi, this is your brother! How can you joke like that?" Kara crossed her arms. "Sometimes you're so insensitive."

"He's fine," Levi said. "We'll get to him, save him, and get the hell outta this crazy place and-"

Flashes of light streaked painfully through his vision, and his head began to pound harder than the rattling coming from below the taxi. The green grass and endless colors of cars outside began to blur and morph together. He couldn't tell where the road ended and the cars began. He blinked hard, clearing his vision long enough to see the first bunch of trees since they'd gotten in the taxi.

"Shit." Levi placed his hands on either side of his head. "Not again."

"Hey," Kara said. "Is it the visions? Hold still, I'll use my magic to-"

Levi pressed his hand against her mouth.

"Shh. You can't use your magic here, yeah? It's just going to have to happen."

"But you-"

Levi blinked a couple of times, realizing he was in the library back in Speyer, his German hometown. He was sitting in a chair, a book in his lap. What was it?

"Schaltungen," Levi murmured. "My circuits class?"

He couldn't remember how long it'd been since he took circuits in college. That was his sophomore year.

As he opened the book, he noticed a note tucked inside. His handwriting scrawled out paragraphs of notes in German, some of which he now struggled to read. It was the reading of another language he had problems with. He could speak it just fine.

One of the paragraphs that he could *read was hastily written, sloppier than the rest. It was coordinates. Dozens of different locations all written in red ink scribbled over and over and over again.*

"Well, well, look what we have here."

Wait.

His eyes went up to Eric's dark brown ones, and he realized that he remembered this scene all too well.

"Eric." Levi slammed the book closed, on cue, just as he'd done before. "I was starting to think you forgot about me."

"Never, Levi," Eric said. "Are you tired of this little game yet? Hm?"

Levi grinned as he stood up and dusted off his pant legs.

Eric was messing with his head by bringing them back to this moment when he almost got caught. But slowly, the details came back to him, and he remembered that he predicted the fact that Eric was near. For some reason, certain parts of Germany gave Eric trouble while tracking him down. He had strayed from one of those areas accidentally the day before, marked by the coordinates written on his paper, so he'd prepared himself for this moment.

"Never. I just hope you have some point to showing me this scene again-"

The knife penetrated his skin, sinking deep and tearing through the very fibers holding him together.

"I-" he cringed as the smell of his blood touched his nose. "T-This isn't how this goes. Y-You don't catch me."

The mark on his back began to burn, and as his eyes traveled up Eric's arm, he saw the black tail on Eric's own mark began to turn red.

"Not this time, huh?"

"No. It's just a vision," Levi repeated over and over. He ground his teeth together as a smile spread across Eric's face. "Th…"

Eric leaned in, his warm breath clouding Levi's face.

"What's that? Are you trying to say something, rat? Speak a little louder."

Levi swallowed back the lump in his throat and grabbed Eric's arm, pushing the knife deeper into his own body and pulling their faces closer together.

"Thunder."

Eric's eyes widened as the library shook, and the hair on both of their arms-

Levi gasped, his eyes bursting open as the cool sensation of Kara's healing magic touched his forehead.

"K-Kara!"

"What the hell is that back there?" the driver asked. The car began to slow. "What are you doing, some kind of-"

Levi lifted his arm and narrowed his eyes. A quick mumble left his lips, and the man turned back around and continued to drive as normal.

"Dammit." Another pain tore through him, this time stemming from his hand. "Sorry, Cerva."

He knew that one was from her. That was what he got for using Vulpes magic, a tribe and God that Cerva wasn't a fan of. He hated them, too, but their magic was pretty useful.

"Are you okay?" Kara grabbed him by his shoulders. "What did you see?"

"Damn idiot's just screwing with me now," Levi said. "He's going after Ollie, but he's still messing with me on the side."

Eric was as skillful as one could get with nightmare magic. Other members of the Lupus tribe could use it, too, but Eric was on a level beyond them. Like Levi, Eric had also learned that he could use magic in which other tribes specialized. At a painful price, of course, unless the god of your tribe and whatever tribe's magic you're trying to use are okay with one another.

But the scary part was that Eric had found a way to form together his nightmare magic and the Mus tribe's memory magic, making for some terrible combinations – like the one he just experienced. There was no telling what other magic he was experimenting with and fusing together.

Levi bit the inside of his cheek, a failed attempt at shoving the surging adrenaline back down in his stomach.

"So, what's going to happen?" Kara's voice was almost too soft to hear. Levi tilted his head. "Are you going to kill him after you save your brother?"

Levi sank back in his seat.

Killing Eric would be…difficult. He owed it to his mother and sister – and father, he guessed – to rid that horrible creature from the earth. But Eric, as he said before, was in a league all his own.

Maybe in a higher one than Levi.

"Well, maybe." Levi rubbed his palms on his pants. "The game of chase is kinda fun. Gives me something to do, you know?"

"Yeah, but aren't you tired?" Kara asked, placing her hand on his. "We could finally go back to Russia and settle down and-"

Levi's phone dinged.

He pulled his hand out from under hers and fished the phone from his pocket. Whatever the alert was, he was relieved. That was an issue he didn't want to discuss right now.

"Let's see, upcoming magician Ol-" Levi jerked the screen closer to his eyes. "Oliver Lee? Oh, god."

"Oliver's on the internet?" Kara pulled the phone away from his face so she could see it. "Upcoming magician Oliver Lee and Nik Rafiel to perform at town hall. Tickets are sold out."

"What…is he doing?" Levi said. "Advertising himself like that. Eric's probably right on top of him."

Kara handed the phone back and sighed.

Whether or not he wanted to talk about it, Levi knew that the time would come when he needed to kill Eric. With the way Oliver was rolling, it was going to have to be sooner rather than later. Like *now* sooner.

But he wasn't ready. He still needed more time to train his power and...

"Dammit, Ollie."

***

As the taxi rolled into the big city, Levi began to recognize the structure of the buildings. Oliver was here, but it was going to take a miracle to find out where. He knew Cerva didn't want him to break the flow of time. She'd instructed him to only intervene after Oliver jumped, but if he found him beforehand...

Well, Cerva would have to be mad at him.

"Looks like we're here. NYU." The taxi driver stopped. "Are you going to pay with cash or..."

Levi mumbled under his breath, and the driver turned back around. Another pain shot through Levi's body.

"Come on." Levi grabbed Kara's arm and pulled her out. "We need to find the building Ollie-"

A loud siren cut through the air, and a police car flew by. In the distance, Levi could hear a megaphone blurting out orders like 'Stay away from the body,' and 'Nothing to see here, folks.'

There was a slim chance that this had anything to do with Oliver, but they had to start somewhere.

"Let's follow them," Levi said. "If nothing else, we'll walk past the building and I'll recognize it."

Unfortunately, that wasn't the case. All the buildings looked the same, and no matter which way he turned, he couldn't find the exact, picture-perfect angle that he'd seen in his vision. As they walked from street to street, the voice grew louder, and soon they were staring at a mob of people all grouped around one spot.

"This is why we need gun control," one man said.

"No, if this man would've had a gun, he'd be fine!"

"Look at him! He's just a child! He shouldn't have a gun!"

Levi wrinkled his nose as both he and Kara pushed past several people. When they got to the front of the group, they saw the *child* lying on the street. He was pale white, and even with his eyes closed, he still had a look of terror on his face. His blonde hair, which was dirty and unkempt, had little splatters of blood originating from the hole in his chest.

"Goodness." Kara's hand squeezed Levi's arm. "Poor kid."

A small vibration came from his pocket, but it wasn't from his phone, which he held firmly in his hand. His fingers closed around the buzzing pocket watch, and when he pulled it out and popped it open, the day was the same, but not the hour.

Megan Ransdell

He clicked the button on the top, and everything around him rushed past. Even Kara, whom he'd forgotten to warn, disappeared, and he was left alone. But not actually, he realized, as he noticed the boy now standing, staring at Levi.

His frost-colored eyes sent a chill down Levi's back as a hint of nostalgia fell over him. They reminded him of-

"Karp."

The boy, Karp, already looked tired, sleep deprived, and terrified, but as this voice – one that they both recognized – said his name, he began to shake. He was now the color of a ghost as he stared at the figure behind Levi.

"S-Sir!" Karp said, and Levi turned to see Eric. "I-I was just-"

Eric held out his hand. Karp's eyes darkened, his face twisted, and he stared off into the sky. He was using his psychic magic from the Vulpes tribe on the kid, just as he'd been doing to Levi these past couple days. Or, was it his nightmare magic? It was hard to tell anymore.

"Stop!" Karp's shrill scream cut through the air as he fell to the ground. "I-I tried! He used his magic! He was too p-powerful."

As Eric walked past Levi, his hand crunched into a fist, making the kid shriek louder. So Eric *had* found a way to form the magic together. That explained how he was able to manipulate Levi's memory in the library.

"I told you to bring him to me," Eric said. "He's just a scrawny Cerva!"

Ollie.

"P-Please…" Karp whimpered. "I-I couldn't convince him to come with me."

Eric's foot came down on Karp's chest, pinning him down as if he was prepared for him to break the magic, jump up, and take off running. His fist loosened and Karp's eyes came back into focus.

"You didn't try hard enough. You wouldn't have brought him to me anyway."

Karp writhed under Eric's foot for a couple of seconds before his head whipped left and right, looking for help. His eyes then fell in Levi's direction.

For a second, Levi wasn't sure if this was the past or the present. This kid appeared to be looking *right at him.* Right into his eyes, begging and pleading with him to intervene. Eric looked his way, too, making Levi's breath catch in his throat, but returned to glaring at Karp.

Finally, Karp released his grip on Eric's shoe. His face was twisted and wrinkled in an expression that made him look older. His eyes were crinkled, but they were calm and hopeless at the same time, almost like he'd predicted this long before.

"B-By my blood, I swear, by my very pain," Karp said, his frost-colored eyes flashing red. "I will follow you everywhere, as a poison among your veins-"

A shard of ice shot from Eric's hand and cut through Karp's chest.

"No," Levi whispered as he watched the life slowly drain from the kid's eyes.

Eric's deep, throaty chuckle bounced off the walls of the building.

"What a waste of-" Eric's voice choked. "What-"

He fell backwards to the ground as he furiously ripped up his right pant leg, revealing several large boils and burns.

"A poison among your veins." Eric's fist slammed the ground. "Dammit!"

The kid had used blood magic. Like low level blood magic from the Mus tribe.

Time stopped and then rushed back forward. Levi felt a grip around his arm, and Kara was suddenly back beside him.

"Goodness," she said. "Poor kid."

Levi's eyes fluttered at the realization that Kara had seen nothing of what he did. To her it was like he'd never left.

"I-I..." Levi backed away from the body. "We need to find Ollie, Kara. Now."

Even while poisoned, Eric's power was…beyond his
comprehension. He'd gotten so good at not only his own tribe's magic,
but all the others', too, that Levi couldn't even tell what kind of magic
he was using. Meanwhile, he was still just trying to perfect *some* of the
Vulpes tribe's abilities. In a head-to-head battle, he would lose just as
easily as this kid had.

This kid… who was alive only hours ago. Eric was coming in
hot with a vengeance, killing anyone and anything that sullied his
plans. If things had gone differently, if he and Kara would've gotten
here at any other time… would they have met Eric head on?

Could this Karp kid have been them?

"Huh?" Kara turned towards him. "I thought we still had a few
days before-"

"W-We do, we just need to find him."

Kara tilted her head.

"Levi," she said. "Are you alright?"

She couldn't know what he saw, the demonstration of power
he'd just witnessed. It would only cause her to panic. Eric was getting
more powerful by the second.

But…things were going to be okay. He could handle it, and he
could find a way out of this. He always did. Granted, he was always
running *away* from Eric and not dancing around him like an ant on
warm pavement.

Shit.

"I'm fine. Come on."

They needed to get Oliver and get out of America as quickly as possible. Oliver would have to learn the game of chase just as Levi did. Except Oliver wouldn't be alone, and he wouldn't have to be scared.

Levi was going to make sure to protect him.

Chapter 4

As Levi attempted to close the door behind him, attention still on the curvy body on his bed, he realized the door was caught again on the stiff brown carpet sticking straight up. Yesterday he'd gotten a little too mad at it catching like this and nearly yanked the door off the hinges while trying close it. Doing so may have made things worse, as it was now torn in multiple places, giving it a sort of hand-shaped grip around the corner of the door.

"Levi, man."

He still hadn't gotten used to understanding Russian entirely. Especially with the people he now hung out with on a regular basis. Bratva, or the Russian mafia, spoke a lot of slang he wasn't used to hearing, making things twenty times harder. He managed, though. It took him forever to learn German, too, but he was fluent in it. Russian would be the same.

Levi shivered as his eyes went up to the ceiling, realizing that yet another large hole had opened up in it, allowing the brisk air to kiss his flushed skin. He buttoned his shirt and crossed his arms in an attempt to stay warm, not yet catching on to his friend's uncharacteristically serious expression.

"Sanya." Levi studied his friend's face. "What's the matter?"

"Some guy," Sanya said. "Think he's a, uh, Chen, you know?"

A relaxing night couldn't be followed with a calm day, could it?

The Chechen was Bratva's rivals. The assholes were always trying to stir up trouble. Ever since Levi took out their leader with his magic, they'd been raging out of control. And so were the police, for that matter.

"Sidor hasn't taken him out yet?" Levi asked.

"Nah, the Chen's been requesting you." Sanya's eyebrows raised. "By name."

There was no way the Chen knew Levi by name. His face was almost entirely covered during the assassination. Even if someone did see him, they'd only recognize him by his face, not his name.

"Now how am I supposed to believe that?" Levi lit a cigarette. "No Chen knows my name."

"Guy's serious about it, Levi," Sanya said. "Older man. Black."

Levi stopped mid-inhale.

A black Chen? Around here? That sounded an awful lot like…

His thoughts began to race, but he shoved them away. He was just being paranoid again. He could not show any fear no matter who it was. Chen or not.

"Fine," Levi said. "I'll check it out."

He pulled on his leather jacket and smoothed back his hair. He didn't care who this guy was, but he needed him gone. He couldn't know him by name.

His eyes lingered on the walls of the old, abandoned house as he followed Sanya through the halls. There were more holes everywhere, either where one of the guys, or girls, got mad and punched through it, or where the black mold had eaten its way through. The ceilings were stained with brown circles from cigarette smoke, if there even was one above the room, and the carpets were outdated, soggy, and ruined.

But it was home.

Sanya and Levi shoved their way past the group of guys, each one holding some form of weapon. Even though Levi knew he didn't need a weapon because he had his magic, he felt oddly exposed. Vulnerable.

"Levi," Sidor said. "Guy says he knows you. Wanted to see you before we killed him."

Levi stopped in his tracks as he took in the sight of the man he'd known since he was a baby. A man that shot fear from his toes, all the way up to the top of his head.

It took him so long to find his voice, that even Sidor turned to him first with confusion, then concern.

"Eric," Levi said. "The hell are you doing here?"

Levi knew what he was doing here, but he couldn't clear his throat enough to say anything else. He was here to collect the very last piece of his puzzle. The last thing he needed before he was to be honored like a god and given the best afterlife he could possibly imagine.

"Hanging with the muck and scum of Russia, are you?" Eric asked. "I'm sure your mother would be proud that you've joined a gang."

"Man, Levi, who's this guy?" Sidor cracked his knuckles. "What's he talking about your mother?"

Levi's fists clenched so hard that it almost hurt.

"One I was telling you about," he said, and all his friends turned to him. "One who killed my family."

Silence fell over the group. They'd all heard the stories. They knew what this meant.

"Hey, man, let me tell you something." Sanya made his way up to Eric, standing a couple inches above him. "You mess with any of my brothers, you're going to get it. And you done messed with one."

The crowd around them muttered in agreement.

"Guys, no, he's different than-"

"Relax, we'll have this guy out in no time," Sidor said. "Regret ever messing with you or Bratva."

Eric's laugh cut through Levi's concentration, and he was soon trying to force the lump down his throat.

"Bratva?" Eric asked. "You're not the mafia. You're just a bunch of kids playing pretend."

"What'd you say, my friend?" Sidor asked. "If you wanna see credentials, I think me and my boys can arrange something."

A couple of the higher ups – the ones who'd been in the group as long as Sidor – stepped forward, guns in hand.

"Sidor, no, you don't-"

Eric's hands rose in slow motion, but it still wasn't enough time for Levi to do anything. He just stood there stunned, like an antelope in the presence of the scariest predator in existence. Even as fire exploded from Eric's palms and the smell of burning flesh and shrill screams filled the air, the only thing that made him move was the force of the blow.

As Levi's back slammed through the wall of the wooden building, a vibration tore through him, and he heard a snap. When he glanced down at his arms, which he used to block his face, pain shot through his body, as well as a sickness in the pit of his stomach. He watched through blurred vision as his blood dripped onto the dirt floors.

"Levi!" Sanya burst through the door. "This...guy. These the kinds of 'abilities' you were telling me about?"

The more Levi watched his blood drip, the more the room began to spin. He put his hand to his head, but it only brought the dripping substance closer.

"Dude, man!" Sanya yelled. "You gotta get out."

"Wha-" Levi shook his head. "I can't leave you all, he's just going to-"

"One of the best things my big brother taught me is that running away's okay sometimes, man." Sanya checked around the door. "Guy's bad news. Get out."

More flames and gunshots filled the air outside.

"H-He's not going to go away." Levi's voice cracked. "I'll just have to keep running."

"Then that's what you gotta do. The strongest man can make the best outta the worst, Levi. Run. Now."

Levi gasped as he breathed in the warm night air. His eyes fluttered, revealing the blurry image of the dark sky and twinkling stars above him. He rubbed his dry, fully healed forearms while he looked around, the memories of checking into a hotel room returning to him.

From the hotel room's balcony he was standing on, he could see dozens of people walking on the sidewalks. But even as hard as he looked, he still couldn't find the one person he so desperately needed.

His eyes went down to aching hands, which he now realized were clenched as tight as they'd go around the railing.

Okay, Levi, relax.

He sighed at the overconfident voice his head. How could he relax when he had to figure out a way to save his brother, avoid Eric, and somehow get out of America?

You've been doing this for years. You'll find a way. You always do.

Yeah, but what was the way? It wasn't just him or him and Kara anymore. It was going to be Oliver, too, and he owed it to his little brother to protect him this time.

"Levi?"

Levi's heart skipped a beat and his adrenaline spiked as he spun around. But it was only Kara. She was standing behind him, her pale skin and snow-white nightgown glowing from the light of the streetlamp outside. He sighed in relief.

"Hey." Levi released the railing. "What are you doing up?"

"I couldn't stop thinking about that poor kid," she whispered. "What could have happened to-"

"Eric."

He refused to make eye contact with her, as he knew she was trying to get him to do. She stared at him expectantly, like he knew all the answers.

"How…do you know?" Kara asked, and her eyes narrowed. "Did you use the watch? What did you see?"

She couldn't know. She couldn't know that this was beyond his capability.

That he was a fake.

"Just that Eric killed him. That's all."

"Are you sure? I know when you're-"

"Kara." Levi grabbed her by the shoulders. "Go back to bed, okay? I'll be there soon."

The two of them glared at each other for what felt like forever.

"I told you we need to stop keeping secrets from each other," she finally said. "I know you're trying act like you have everything under control, but…"

"I *do* have everything under control," Levi said. "I used the watch, Eric killed him, that's all I saw, yeah?"

What would she say to him if she knew how much of a phony he was? How even though he'd trained countless hours for the very moment they were in, he still wasn't strong enough?

"Why do you do this?" Kara asked. "Why do you insist on-"

"Kara. Enough," Levi snapped. "If there was something you needed to know, I'd tell you. I don't know what you want me to say."

Her fists were balled up and her jaw was clenched, but as Levi's eyes narrowed, in an almost 'I dare you' fashion, she huffed.

"Fine."

She yanked her shoulders from his arms and went back inside, burying herself deep underneath the blankets and comforter.

Nice one, Levi.

He let out a low growl at his inner voice.

Okay. You've got this. You're not a fake, and you're going to get away from this guy.

No, he was a fake. He'd spent half of his life running from Eric and never facing him head on. He acted like this was a game, but really it was a desperate attempt at preserving his life the only way he knew how. And sure, he was okay at magic, but he was okay for a Cerva. That wasn't saying much, he knew. The Cerva weren't known for their fighting abilities. Besides his mother, that was.

She was the most powerful person from the tribe, yet she still couldn't stop Eric.

Yeah, but what about that one battle you had with psycho Eric? When you mortally injured him?

Levi snorted. It wasn't mortally enough, apparently.

Okay, look. Get little Ollie, get Kara, go to Germany, hide out. It's that easy. You don't need the rest planned out. Since when does Levi plan things out?

Since he'd found out his little brother was in trouble.

Okay. Fair point. But it worked up to this point. Why wouldn't it now?

Levi nodded. As sad as it seemed, that made a lot of sense. He was still alive and pretty much as happy as he could get. That was from not planning for the last eight years. Actually, probably his whole life, now that he thought about it.

There was no need to worry. As long as he stayed cool and collected, he would get done what needed to get done.

Chapter 5

Or not.

"Dammit, dammit, dammit."

Levi slammed his fist into the plaster wall of the hotel room. It'd been three days and still nothing. New York wasn't as tiny as it looked on a map. How could he still not have found Oliver yet?

Keep your cool, dude.

He grabbed the lamp from the side table and flung it towards the floor, cracking it in several pieces. Keeping his cool hadn't helped him yet, so why should he? He paced back and forth between the hole and broken lamp.

"You know we're going to have to pay for those, right?" Kara crossed her arms.

Levi pressed his forehead against the wall. His little brother was about to jump off a building today, and it was already two o'clock.

"Where could he be?" he mumbled. "He's a foreign guy in the middle of America. You'd think he'd be easier to spot."

"Well, New York is the 'melting pot' of America."

Levi rolled his eyes as he made his way back out to the balcony. There was no way he was going to track down Oliver in a matter of hours when he couldn't even do it in a matter of days.

Panic washed over him as he gazed down at the streets below. All he could see were strangers. Even the birds were unrecognizable to the ones he knew in Germany and Russia. America was such a strange place.

The way people moved, the way they talked...it was all overwhelmingly different. The only thing he found comfort in, which was weird, was the broken infrastructure of the buildings around him. There were tons of crappy buildings around the area where he lived in Russia. Actually, he lived in a couple of them.

Even the nicer apartments across the street had problems. Their door, which was completely crunched in, was unusable. How was anyone supposed to-

The watch in his pocket vibrated, and when he pulled it out and popped it open, the time only showed a five-minute difference.

"What?" He pressed the button.

The time frame was too short for him to see the scene backwards per usual. Instead, the door was suddenly fixed, and before he could blink-

It burst open, and Oliver stumbled out. He turned, almost tripping over his own feet, mumbled something, and the door caved in. He stepped a couple of paces backwards, his face unreadable, and took off running.

From the back of the building, a full minute after, Eric emerged from another door. He rubbed his cheek, and then his right leg, before limping around the building and taking his time in the same direction as Oliver.

"No," Levi said as time jumped back forward. "Dammit!"

Kara poked her head out, her eyebrows pressed together. "Levi?"

"I'm such an idiot! He's been in the apartments right across the street." Levi shook his head. "Come on. We need to go."

He grabbed Kara's hand and they sprinted down the halls and stairs.

Whoa, whoa, Levi. Remember. Calm. Stay calm and everything's going to work.

He shook his voice out of his head. He knew he needed to stay calm, dammit.

As they ran down the sidewalks and darted through the streets, Levi tried to think of where Oliver might be headed. He'd run out of the building by himself. The blue-haired girl wasn't with him. Could she be at the college? Would that be where he was running?

Levi stopped in the middle of the sidewalk. The scene he saw was now well over ten minutes ago. Oliver would've already made it to NYU if that's where he was going.

"Where is he, Levi?"

He shook his head. He needed to concentrate. He needed time to-

"Lynn?" Levi's eyes shot up at the round man shouting. "Don't go in there!"

A blue-haired girl, who he now recognized as the girl with Oliver, rushed past the man. Was that the hotel clerk? Levi knew Eric mentioned something about the two of them going together to find Oliver and Lynn, but he figured Eric would've already killed him by now.

"There." Levi ran towards the building after the clerk rushed in. "Kara, I need you to be on the roof in five. Get whoever you can, okay?"

Kara nodded as she ran inside.

His eyes went up and down the building. It was huge, just like the one in his vision, and the surrounding environment… there was the lone tree between one-way roads, the strange, off-blue, shorter building. This was it. How was he going to get up there, get his brother, and also avoid Eric without messing up the forthcoming events that Cerva had showed him, though?

Dammit. Think!

He shook his head. The heat of the moment would bring him an idea. Just as his thoughts had told him earlier.

He sucked in a deep breath and continued toward the door, but just as he was also about to get in, he ran into a tall, well-dressed younger man who looked about his own age.

"I'm so sorry, sir," the man said, clutching a Bible to his chest. "While you're here, would you like to hear a word or two about our Lord-"

"No, no, just get out of-" Levi's eyes zeroed in on the book in the man's hands, and just like that, he had an idea. "Well, actually, gimme that."

He didn't give the man enough time to respond after he ripped the book from his hands and entered the building. On the stairwell above, he could hear stomping and banging.

Levi stopped on the third floor, his heart racing so fast he was scared it might leap out.

He couldn't go up there. That would mean him interfering with the vision he'd seen, and Cerva would be pissed. Plus, that would mean a direct confrontation in the middle of New York on top of a building full of families. Eric wasn't afraid to demonstrate his power in front of people without magic.

As Levi searched the hall, his gaze stopped on a door that had a cross proudly displayed right square in the middle of it.

Bingo.

He knocked on the door, and within a few seconds, an old black woman opened it.

"Hello?" Her voice had a heavy southern accent.

"Hello, ma'am," Levi said, making sure the Bible he held was in plain sight. He had to make a conscious effort to make his words come out calm and even. "Do you have a minute to talk about God?"

A surprised smile touched her wrinkled, sun-dried face.

"Well, of course I do, honey." She held the door open for him. "Come in, have a seat. Did you kid's Bible class downstairs get canceled?"

The room had nice, light-brown carpeting, with contrasting darker brown walls that made the area look small and cozy. Just ahead of them were three arm couches, all of which matched the brown color scheme of her room. But that pot in the corner of her room, an offensive blue when compared to her otherwise perfect design, looked familiar somehow. Where had he-

He shook his head.

"Yeah, that's it. I'll sit here, if I may." Levi motioned to the chair facing the window before sitting down. "We normally like to start by talking about our favorite verse, if you don't mind."

Contrary to what one might believe, Levi actually had read the Bible, so he knew exactly which line to reference. He'd read a lot of different religious texts, honestly. He enjoyed the idea of religion and what it had to offer, and he always found himself grabbing for stuff like this at libraries.

He waited with patient anxiety as she shuffled, almost like she was wearing skis, toward one of the arm couches.

"This is Ezekiel 45:9," he continued. "Do you know it?"

He knew what he needed to do, but it was something he'd never tried before. He'd used this kind of magic in other situations with other things, but...

His eyes went to his shaking hands. He tensed to keep them still before the lady could notice. She was taking her dear, sweet time to sit down.

"Of course I do, honey-" A loud crashing sound, followed by a couple of thuds above their heads, made the woman's eyes widen. "What…what was that-"

"I love this verse. Thus says the Lord GOD, 'Enough, you princes of Israel; put away violence and destruction, and practice justice and righteousness.'" Levi held out his hand towards the window as he inhaled a deep breath. "'*Stop*…your expropriations from My people,' declares the Lord GOD."

Nothing happened for the longest time, and for a second, Levi realized he might've been too late.

His heart was in his throat, and his brain went silent. The woman's eyebrows pressed together as she stared at his frozen expression.

But suddenly, an invisible force came down on him, the weight almost too heavy for him to hold. His eyes tore reluctantly from the book. He didn't know what he was about to see, but…there he was.

Floating limp outside the window, held up only by a spell that stopped any kind of motion, was Oliver.

The woman followed his gaze, and her eyes nearly popped from their sockets.

"Goodness gracious!" she said. "What in the name of all that's holy-"

Levi rushed forward and threw open the window. Oliver's body was close, but still several feet away, and as Levi reached forward, the liquid from his stomach felt like it was in his throat. His fingertips grazed Oliver's brown, long-sleeved shirt as he felt his own body shift a little too far forward. As he steadied himself, his brother's body nearly took a nosedive, but as Levi clenched his teeth, Oliver stabilized. He was upside down, but he was secure.

"Pull him in, pull him in!" the old lady shrieked from behind him. He'd almost forgotten she was still there.

Levi swallowed the lump in his throat and leaned forward once more.

Don't look down, don't look down, don't look...

His eyes shot down in morbid curiosity, and the instant he once again saw how high he was, Oliver's body dropped another inch.

"Dammit!" Levi lunged forward and snatched up his brother's hand just as his spell dropped.

His lower body braced against the window ceil as he took in a deep breath and yanked his brother's upper half into the room. Finally, with one more heave, his brother toppled over him and halfway onto one of the armchairs.

"How did you-" The lady was standing now. "How did you do that?"

"Uh." Levi panted as he lifted his brother over his shoulder. "'With God all things are possible.' Matthew 19:26?"

As he opened the door, Kara was there, the blue-haired girl over her shoulder. His presence startled her, and she jumped a couple of feet in the air.

"Levi!" she said, and her eyes fell on Oliver. "You got him."

"Come on. We have to go fast, yeah?" Levi turned back to the older woman. "You can keep the Bible. My treat."

"God has sent you to Earth because you're his prophet, young man!" He heard the lady holler. "Please, come back! Forgive me for I have sinned!"

His adrenaline was pumping as he went down the stairs with such expertise that he was sure he was flying down them. As they shoved through the door, Levi felt…this sensation, but as he turned around, it was too late.

He shielded his brother's body as best as he could from the incoming fire, and the only thing that saved his own body from being scorched was the wind spell he used last second. It sent both he and Oliver flying down the sidewalk.

"Wow." Eric's voice filled Levi's ears as he pushed himself from the ground. "Who would've thought?"

"Eric," Levi forced out. "It's been a while."

A trickling sensation from his elbow caught his attention, and as he grudgingly stole a glance down at his arm, he felt his stomach knot.

"I never get tired of the look on your face when you see your own blood," Eric said. "But it's crazy. I thought you'd be a little more prepared for that attack. You normally are, aren't you?"

"Shut up." Levi said. "You-"

He shook away his blurred vision as he strained to see the image in front of him.

"Admit it, rat. You're falling apart."

"Falling apart and you still haven't managed to catch me." Levi laughed, flinging the blood from his arm. "And you're not going to."

"Not going to? Why, I have you right here."

Levi's eyes widened as Eric held out his hand – an all too familiar move.

"Not this time," Levi growled.

The ground shook, and as Levi took in a deep breath, water came gushing from the fountain beside them. There were gallons underneath the ground, Levi could feel, and it'd be just enough for what he planned to do.

The water moved with his arm – a skill that took years of practice and control – and flew forward towards Eric. It was torrential as it sucked him in without mercy.

"Freeze." Levi closed his hand into a fist.

The water crystalized, and soon, an ice sculpture stood at least twenty feet tall in the middle of the sidewalk.

See? Not a fake.

Levi grinned.

That was actually a lot easier than he thought it would be. Maybe it was the poison the kid had blessed him with, or maybe Eric was growing old and was off *his* game. Whatever the case, this was going great.

"Is he..." Kara's voice was shaky. "Is he d-"

Slowly, and Levi stood there every daunting second of it, a path in the ice melted, and Eric was standing there unharmed and unphased.

"Kara," Levi said in an even voice. "Can you carry Ollie, too?"

As if Kara could read his mind, her face twisted into a scowl.

"Levi, you can't-"

"Can you carry Ollie, too?" he interrupted, and Kara nodded. "Get him out of here, yeah? I'll catch up."

The sky darkened, and rumbles sounded in the distance.

"But..."

"Go, Kara." His eyebrows pressed together. "Please."

Her body transformed in front of him from her beautiful, slender figure to a built, handsome man as she heaved Oliver off the ground. She glanced back at him, her mouth hanging open like she wanted to say something, but she soon disappeared into the distance.

"Hey! Hands up!" Police cars screeched to a halt in front of the building and armed officers poured through the door. "Hands up you two or we'll-"

Levi's eyes followed the line of officers, and they were all soon getting back in their cars and leaving the scene. Even the bystanders began walking away.

"I see you've been dabbling with Vulpes magic," Eric said. "That's pretty good. I'd have to say that, besides myself, you're the most skilled in magic I've ever seen."

"You give me too much credit," Levi snorted. "I saw what you did to that kid. He poisoned you, huh?"

Eric pulled up his pant leg to reveal the nasty, oozing sores on his leg. Levi could tell by Eric's shortness of breath and clenched jaw that it was having an effect on him.

"Nothing I can't handle. He was of the Mus tribe, but his magic was weak."

"I'm not going to let you get Ollie," Levi said. "You're not going to get either of us."

Eric smiled as he rose back up. He looked so confident, so sure of himself.

"What, are you going to keep running?" he asked. "This game's getting old, Levi. You're eventually going to have to face your fears."

"I'm not scared of you."

"Your shaking legs say otherwise." Eric laughed as Levi locked his knees. "What's the matter? Don't think you can match up? Or is it the blood?"

Levi glanced down at his arm once more to see the blood dripping from his fingertips. He shook his head as his vision blurred again.

"Is it that you know if you die, your little brother doesn't stand a chance?" Even though Eric was coming towards him, Levi couldn't find the strength to move his legs. "That he'd be just like your mother and little sister? Are you afraid you can't save him either?"

"Don't," Levi said as Eric neared him. "I know what you're going to do, don't-"

Eric held out his hand and Levi squeezed his eyes shut.

"Macie, baby, come on. We need to get back home, okay? It's going to be dark soon."

"Mom, why don't we get to leave home more often?"

Levi's eyes widened at the sight of his mother. Her long black hair flowed down her back, free of the usual tight braid she wore. The entirety of her face was covered in some sort of makeup that made the mark on her cheek invisible. But as she looked up towards the grassy field, her dark green eyes were the same. They were deep and calm, wise and strong.

Macie looked almost dead up like her. Her hair was cut short, though, and when she brushed a strand of it behind her ear, he observed the gloves on her hands. That was where her mark was, he remembered. Her brown eyes went to their mother when she didn't answer.

"Oh. Because..." Their mother paused. "It's just complicated, honey."

"Where's Levi?"

Levi's ears perked.

"What?" Their mom shook her head.

"He's been gone for an awful long time again. Why does he keep leaving? Do you think he's going to come back?"

For a brief second, when his mother's eyes fell on him, he thought she could see him. But when her expression didn't change, and the darkness in her eyes didn't fade, he realized that she was merely keeping a close eye on her surroundings.

His heart dropped to his stomach. This was the second time he'd been fooled by the visions. What was making him suddenly confuse them with reality?

"I...I don't know, baby. I sure hope he does."

Levi shook his head as he backed away. He couldn't see this again. He couldn't handle the-

A tree branch cracked, and their mother spun on her heels.

"Who-" Terror streaked her face for only a split second. "Eric? No."

"Hello, dear." Eric stepped from the forest. "It's about time I found you again."

"Mom, who's-"

Their mother stepped forward and shoved Macie behind her. Her eyes were narrowed, and her strong, warrior-like stance was one he faintly remembered from a time long ago.

"Macie, run home. Don't stop." She wiped the side of her face, revealing her mark. "Fire!"

A string of fire, much like the one he saw in his vision of Oliver, shot from her hand and barely missed Eric.

Her moves were dance-like as she took on Eric with fiery palms, attempting to land a direct hit through his chest. He tried the same with her, but they were both unsuccessful as they responded immediately to one another's every move, breath, and facial expression. They fought like they knew the other's every thought process. Like they knew the other more than anyone else.

However, his mom became disoriented for only a second, if that, but it was enough for Eric to get the best of her, sending her to the ground. His foot came down on her chest, pinning her in place.

"No," she huffed. They stared into one another's eyes for a long time, as if trying to figure the other out. "Y-You're not going to... I-"

A shard of ice went through her chest, like with Karp, and her ragged breathing came to a halt.

"No!" Levi yelled, but he couldn't move his legs. "Mom!"

"Mom? Mommy!" Macie came running from behind a tree. "Get off of her! What did you do? Mom!"

"Macie, no! Don't…" Tears ran down Levi's face. "Macie…"

Eric allowed Macie to shove his foot from her mother and sob for a couple of minutes over her body. He even walked away and stared up at the clouds, almost like he was looking for some kind of praise within them.

He eventually turned back around and return to the two of them as Macie continued to yell and shake their mom's body.

"S-Stay away. Stay a-" Eric knotted his hand in Macie's hair as she cried out in pain and tried to pull away. "M-M-Mom."

"Don't," Levi said when he saw Eric pull his knife out. "Eric. Eric, I swear I'll fucking-"

Levi's eyes came back into focus as soon as the knife pierced his sister's chest.

"Well, rat," Eric whispered. "Had enough?"

Levi's hands were shaking. He couldn't stop them like he had with his legs. But as he tore his attention up, he realized Eric's face was inches from his. He could make out every line on Eric's skin, every scar, and his eyes…they held a fire in them that made Levi's insides light up.

He chuckled as Eric continued to glare down at him.

"I've only just begun, my friend," he said, and the sky rumbled again. "Thunder."

Chapter 6

The soft, metallic *tzzt, tzzt, tzzt* of the cymbal came first.

It was almost too quiet to hear for a while, but after a couple of minutes, it was clear as day. A guitar entered next, bouncing the swinging melody seamlessly to a piano. They crescendoed slowly together, but not too much.

Now just the guitar strummed for a while, picking through a series of scales and arpeggios, the piano doing the same when it was its turn. They both cut out so the cymbal, which had been long forgotten as anything but a background noise, and the drums could take the spotlight. The music crescendoed again, every instrument playing at this time.

Then, a simple bridge back to the beginning so it could unfold all over again.

The same way. Nothing different.

It was like some form of musical purgatory that was inescapable. The steady beat floated you from the ground and refused to let you go anywhere. Over, and over, and over again. Repeating dynamics. Identical notes and tones. It was almost as if it had been written in the script to do exactly what was written. No more, no less. It was agonizing the way-

Oliver gasped for air and gripped his throat as his eyes burst open. He was met with the strange grey walls of an unfamiliar room.

"What?" His head whipped both ways before he threw the comforter from his body and nearly fell off the bed. "Where-"

"Oliver! Hey! Shh, shh. Calm down."

His eyes met the blue ones of a tiny, pale, blond girl standing in the doorway.

"Look, I know you must be scared but-" Her voice cut off as Oliver shoved past her and into another room. "Hey? Hey!"

He could remember shoving Mr. Bain back with his wind magic, which also sent himself backwards. He was going to save his brother from being hunted, he was finally going to be free, too. But more importantly, he remembered Lynn getting put to sleep by Mr. Bain's magic. What if Oliver hadn't shoved him far enough? What if he had taken Lynn and-

Lying on the couch was Lynn's soft, sleeping body. Her chest rose slowly with each breath she took, and the way her eyes, lips, and cheeks snuggled into the cushion almost made him calm again.

"Oliver, listen to me," the girl said. "You need to calm down-"

"Who are you?" Oliver backed away. "Where are we? Where's Mr. Bain?"

His eyes widened as he realized that he wasn't dead. He'd shoved himself off but he'd somehow survived. He couldn't remember hitting the ground at all, but his arm hurt a lot, like it'd been popped out of place but then put back. But wait, could he be dead right now? Was this the afterlife? His gaze went to the closed curtains, which blew open as he summoned his wind magic once more. This didn't look like the afterlife. It still looked like New York.

"Whoa, stop. I know you have a lot of questions, but I just need you to sit down and-"

Lynn rose from the couch, shaking her head as she rubbed her eyes.

"Oliver?" she asked sleepily, but then her voice shifted to panic. "Oh my god. Oliver?"

She stood up as she looked at both him and the strange girl across the room.

"Okay, good morning. I need you both to-"

"Who the hell are you?" Lynn asked, stepping in front of Oliver. "If you come near him, I swear to God I'll break your fucking nose."

The girl's jaw clenched as she sighed. Then, without warning, her body began to morph, and *she* was suddenly…a *he?*

"What-" Oliver put his hand to his forehead. "What's going on?"

"Look, if you guys don't calm down, I'm going to knock you both back out," the…boy said. "Sit down. Shut up. Listen to me."

"I'd like to see you try," Lynn growled. "Take one more step. I dare you to-"

The front door slammed shut, and everyone froze.

Oliver's mind raced at the thought of Mr. Bain. Had he and this girl found some way to catch him and Lynn and take them somewhere to be tortured before they were killed? If there was one thing Mr. Bain loved, it was tormenting Oliver. Messing him up bad and then leaving him for a while before doing it all over again.

"Hey, everybody calm down, yeah? It's going to be okay."

Oliver's breath caught in his throat.

The voice that filled his ears wasn't Mr. Bain's at all. It was deep and smooth, light and relaxed. One that yanked thousands of memories forward into Oliver's mind with only a single syllable. It brought him comfort, but it also made his heart drop.

His brain felt like it was on fire as it screamed the identity of the person behind him, but he refused to believe it.

There was no way that after all this time…

As he turned, he realized the darkness he was seeing was from the fact that his eyes were squeezed shut. No matter how hard he tried, even when his body stopped, he couldn't pry them open even a little.

Finally, he felt a hand on his shoulder. It was warm as it tightened around him, allowing his eyes to relax. As he took in a deep breath, they fluttered open.

"Hey there, buddy."

Standing before him…the messy, black hair, the shorter, built body…

"Y-You…" Oliver rubbed his eyes to make sure he wasn't dreaming. "L-Levi?"

"Ollie."

It happened all at once. The wall holding everything back, bulging from being so full, burst. Oliver's heart swelled as tears ran down his face and he closed the space between himself and his brother, just as he had when they were kids and Levi would come home after being away for so long. But this time, as he pulled Levi into a hug, he found that his arms were able to hold him tighter. They were able to wrap around him more so than they were eight years ago. He also had to hunch over as he rested his chin on his brother's firm shoulder.

Oliver felt Levi's arms wrap around him, too, almost strangling him.

"O-Oh my god! Your arm's bleeding!" Lynn said.

Oliver pulled away and looked down at his brother's arms, noticing the one on the left trickling blood onto the white carpet.

"Oh." Levi's laugh was weak. "It's still going, huh?"

As Oliver observed him closer, he noticed how different his brother looked from when he last saw him so long ago. He was so confident and sure. No longer did he seem pained and desperate, untrusting and defeated.

But he also looked hardened. Even though he had fresh bruises and cuts on his face and arms, it didn't seem to bother him. Oliver wondered if that meant he'd outgrown his phobia of-

"Shit." Levi stumbled backwards into the arms of the…man. "Kara, I need…"

"It's okay," Kara said, his body morphing back into a woman. "Lie down, I'll fix it."

"How are you doing that?" Lynn asked.

Oliver watched as Kara laid his brother on the couch. She put her hands above his left arm, whispered something elegant and smooth, and soon enough a green light formed between her palm and Levi's elbow.

"Hey," Oliver said, observing the mark on her neck. It looked like his, except it was green and only had one tail on the top, which came off to a leaf shape end. "Um, that mark."

"I'm a Silvan, if you're wondering," Kara said. The gash on Levi's arm began to fade. "And about the other thing, I'm a shifter. I can change my gender. A lot of Silvans can."

Silvan? What was a Silvan? He hadn't the faintest idea, but he knew it probably had something to do with Cerva and his own mark. Were there other tribes besides Cerva and Lupus?

"Ollie," Levi said. "Come here, buddy."

Without a second of hesitation, Oliver was on his knees by the couch. He leaned in close to his brother, who was cringing from pain.

"Are you okay?" He put his hand on top of Oliver's head. "You're not hurt, are you?"

"Well, I…" Oliver laughed as he shook his head, attempting to rid the tears from his eyes. "Y-You're the one who's hurt. I'm fine."

"Oh, I'm fine, too. Just a little blood. You know how I am with that."

Oliver watched with worried eyes as Kara continued to heal his brother's wounds. He didn't know how he'd sustained them – the bruises on his face, the black burn marks on his hands…

"Wait," Oliver said. "Mr. Bain. How…where'd he go?"

"Eric?" Levi asked, and Oliver nodded. "He's taken care of for a while. Don't worry about it. You don't have to anymore."

"Levi, um," Kara said. "The burns on your hand, I can't do anything about-"

"I know."

Oliver's eyebrows wrinkled as he turned his brother's hand over to closer inspect the burns. They kind of looked the same as a tree did when it got struck by lightning, but…

"I'm fine, bud." Levi's fingers curled against his palm. "Hey, I know that-"

"Dad! My dad!" Lynn gasped. "Where's my dad at? Oh my god!"

"I-I'm sorry," Kara said. "You were the only one I could carry off the roof."

Oliver squeezed his eyes shut as he tried to remember what happened right before he jumped off the roof. He remembered Mr. Bain had put Lynn and her dad to sleep…or did he dream that? He wasn't sure. He'd almost forgotten Mr. Bain could use magic. It was so hard to connect the little boy in his visions to the man he'd been working for the past three years.

"We have to go back and get him!" Lynn said. "We can't just leave him there with that psycho. We need to go now and-"

"Whoa, whoa, whoa, lady," Levi said, pushing himself into a sitting position. "We're not going back. No way."

Lynn stomped towards him as she threaded her fingers in her hair.

"What? We…but my dad's there, he's going to kill him-"

"He's probably already dead."

"Levi!" Kara said.

"I'm just being realistic."

Oliver felt Lynn's hand wrap around his, and she squeezed it tight. When he looked over at her, he realized it was a silent hint for him to jump in and back her up.

"Oh! Um, well, Levi," Oliver said. "We can't leave her dad. We gotta get him."

"Oh, no, we don't. Look, Ollie," Levi said. "Here's what's going to happen. You, me, and Kara are all going to Germany, yeah? For some reason Eric has a hard time finding us in-"

"What? But what about Lynn?" Oliver shook his head. "I'm not leaving her, and we can't leave her dad."

"No, we're leaving. She stays-"

Lynn released Oliver's hand.

"You're just going to run away?" she asked. "Oliver's told me all about you. You're so good with magic, yet you're too scared to-"

"Excuse me?" Levi laughed. "Listen, lady. First, I'm not scared of anyone, yeah? And second, you don't have a say so in this. It doesn't concern you."

"It does concern me! He has my dad! You can't just make a mess without cleaning it up!"

When Levi stood from the couch, Oliver watched helplessly as Lynn got up in his brother's face, and they continued to argue. He wanted to say something, but he didn't want to seem like he was taking anyone's side. Lynn was right when she said they couldn't just leave, but Oliver hadn't seen Levi in *eight years.* If he made him mad, what if he left?

Oliver shook his head. He needed to stop them. Everyone was so confused and worked up that things were never going to get solved. Plus, all the yelling. He couldn't stand all the yelling.

"S-Stop," Oliver said, but no one paid him any attention. He felt his face beginning to get hot, and his voice was now louder than he knew it could go. "Hey! I said stop right now!"

Levi, Kara, and Lynn all stared at him, mouths agape.

"I can't…" Oliver had no idea what to say next. "I-I just can't be around this."

He pushed his way past the three of them into the other room, through the balcony doors, and out onto the balcony.

He needed fresh air, and he needed time to think. The last time he'd had an opportunity for any of those things was right before he jumped off the rooftop. He didn't know how many days it'd been since then, but it felt like forever.

Oliver sighed as he leaned over the railing.

He shouldn't have yelled at them and stormed out. How immature was that? It just reminded him of what he used to hear every single day on the ship. It was always utter chaos because *someone* wasn't doing something right. If it wasn't Mr. Bain yelling at him and the others, it was someone else. Like James. It was always someone or something.

His pressed his forehead to the cold rail. He was such an idiot. He hadn't seen his brother in so long, and one of the first things he did was get angry at him. Just as their father seemed to do every time Levi came back home after being gone for days or months.

"Hey, Ollie?"

Oliver gasped as he turned, still not used to the sound of his brother's voice.

"H-Hey." Oliver's eyes went to the ground. "I'm sorry, I shouldn't have-"

"No, stop. It was my fault," Levi said, slowly making his way to Oliver's side. "I'm normally better at keeping my cool than that. I know you hate fighting. You always have."

Oliver nodded as he looked over his brother. Levi was only a little shorter than he was now. Probably about an inch. It was strange, because Levi always used to be the taller one when they were younger.

"I-I can't leave her," Oliver said. "Not at least until I can get her dad back."

Levi's eyebrows pushed together, and his face twisted in a way Oliver wasn't sure he'd seen from his brother. It almost looked like panic, but that didn't make any sense. He'd been so calm just a second ago. His brother stared at him for the longest time.

"Ollie, this is…a life or death situation, buddy," Levi said. "Don't let this girl that doesn't matter get you killed."

"S-She matters to me." Oliver gave his brother a pleading look. "Please, Levi. I messed this up for her. Let me fix it. Please."

Levi turned and leaned over the railing. He said nothing for the longest time.

"Do you remember Macie?" he finally asked. "Remember how she had hair like Mom's?"

Oliver was silent until his brother looked over at him, awaiting his response.

"Um, yeah," Oliver said. "Mom wanted it to grow out and used to brush it for her constantly. But Macie eventually cut it herself because she hated it."

"Do you remember her eyes?"

Oliver tilted his head. He had no idea what his brother was talking about. How did he start thinking about Macie when they were talking about Lynn and her dad?

"Yeah? They were brown," Oliver said, unsure when Levi motioned for him to continue. "And big...they used to kind of shine a little bit when the sun touched them. It always helped her get away with things because they were so sweet."

"I don't remember that. She was only eight when I left for the last time," Levi said. "Eric showed me the day he killed her and Mom. Multiple times. While I was fucking around in Russia, he was putting another two notches in his belt. All I can see when I imagine Macie is him grabbing her by her hair, her big eyes puffy and red from sobbing...and then the tortured pain in them when he stabbed her."

Even though they were outside and the air around them was endless, Oliver couldn't manage to get a breath in.

"W-Why are you telling me this?"

"Because I don't want that to be you, Ollie." Levi's hands wrapped around his brother's shoulders. "I didn't have the chance to protect Mom or Macie. But I can protect you."

"But...your magic's powerful. If Mr. Bain won't give Mason back, you can use your magic to make him."

Levi's hands dropped from his shoulders as he shook his head.

"No, I can't. We've been playing cat and mouse for a reason, you know," he said. "I've practiced and learned so much. Had people tell me I was gifted, intelligent, *powerful*...but it's not enough. It's never been enough. He's always been miles ahead of me."

Oliver stared at the ground. If it wasn't for him, Lynn's dad would be fine. They wouldn't be in this mess. What if he wouldn't have gotten in that fight with the man in Massachusetts? Or followed Lynn back to the hotel?

But he did. *He* was the cause of all this.

"It's okay that you couldn't save Mom and Macie, you know. It's in the past now, and you didn't know it was going to happen. No one did," Oliver said, and Levi's eyes shot up to his. "But we *can* save Lynn's dad. I-I just need your help."

He promised Lynn that they'd get through things. That was when she was talking about her drug problem, but he meant it even afterwards. They traveled to New York, figured out about the Cerva tribe, and watched his magic grow *together*. He wasn't going to leave her like this.

"Do you love her, Ollie?"

"What?" Oliver's eyes fluttered. "D-Do I..."

Levi smiled weakly as he put his arm around Oliver's shoulders. He stared out into the sky, his eyes distant, like he was thinking hard about something. Oliver wanted to ask, but he had no idea how.

"Well, she…" Oliver paused. "She understands me, and she makes me think things through. She's smart and…and funny and… well, she makes me feel like me. D-Does that make sense?"

"Huh."

"F-For the first time in my life I feel like someone accepts me for who I am," he continued softly. "The things I'm carrying with me… well, they don't matter."

Oliver wasn't sure what the expression on his brother's face was, but it almost reminded him of his own while he was on the ship. It was helpless, torn.

"I guess that's a yes," Levi said. "Okay. I'll do it. I'll help you get this lady's dad back."

"Really?"

"Yeah. Yeah, you know… everyone's been saying it, but I just keep denying it." Levi put his hands back on the railing. "It's finally time to end this damn game of chase. It's apparently the only way I'm going to be able to protect you."

Oliver smiled as he joined his brother, staring out into the dark blue sky.

"We're strong enough," he said. "Together."

"Together."

Chapter 7

As Levi and his brother returned to the room, he could see that Kara and Lynn had been talking quietly about something but stopped the moment the door opened. He was surprised, because Kara wasn't normally very good with new people. She was extremely introverted, contrary to how she acted sometimes.

"Alright. We're going to save your dad," Levi said. "But in order to do that we have to kill Eric. There's no other way."

"Wait, we're going to *kill* him?"

Levi's eyes fluttered a couple of times at his brother.

"Uh, Ollie, didn't we just talk about this? Like five seconds ago?"

Lynn and Kara just stared at the two of them, waiting for an answer.

"Oh, um, I mean." Oliver scratched at his collarbone, revealing half of his mark. "But do we really have to *kill* him? Doesn't that make us just as bad as him?"

Levi couldn't believe what he was hearing. Was his little brother this naïve? After seeing Eric kill their mom and sister again and again, Levi wanted nothing more than to see than the life completely drained from the damned Lupus's body.

"Have you forgotten what he's done to us?" he asked. "He made us *suffer.* He's still doing it! I told you, it's time to end this damn game forever."

"Well, Levi, if they really don't want to kill him, there's another-"

"No, Kara, there isn't. There's one way, and it's that he has to die, yeah?" Levi growled. "Now here's the plan. We need to lure him out while he's still injured. If Ollie and I are in the same place at the same time, he won't pass up the opportunity, even if he's hurt."

When no one said anything, Levi's eyebrows furrowed. Kara's face was twisted into an extremely displeased frown, probably because he'd interrupted her. Lynn's was almost the same as Kara's, but for some reason she had this almost bored look to her. He didn't quite understand it. Oliver's, on the other hand, was worried. Levi could tell his mind was racing.

"If there's multiple ways to do this, shouldn't we hear them all and then decide which one's best?" Lynn crossed her arms. "Maybe killing him isn't the easiest solution."

Levi fought back the rage bubbling under his skin. He wasn't *angry,* but when it came to Eric, no one knew more than he did. Levi spent years avoiding the guy and learning where exactly his weak spots were. He'd never taken something so seriously before in his whole life.

"It *is* the easiest solution. But there are two other ways, I guess," he said. "One of them, what Ollie was trying to do earlier, is for someone in the family to kill themselves and prevent the Lupus from completing the family tree. The third one is to seal his mark and magic away. Which we can't do."

The other two ways were ridiculously idiotic. Yes, Levi had considered killing himself just to piss Eric off and protect Oliver if his mark ever appeared, but that was a long time ago. It wouldn't have done anyone any good. The third option, the one he and Oliver's dad wanted to do back when both their parents were still alive, was more than likely the reason their family was dead now.

"Why can't we seal his mark and magic away?" Oliver asked. "That actually sounds better than, well, killing anyone."

Levi's eyes narrowed as he remembered their dad saying the exact same thing.

"No, we have to kill him. I can't do this anymore!"

Levi made sure to stay hidden behind the wall just enough that he could see what was going on but also not be seen. His dad was pacing back and forth in front of his mom as she clenched and unclenched her fists.

"Charlie, we can't. He's another human being," his dad said. "I've read through everything. I can seal his power away-"

"He killed my family. My friends." She grabbed his father by the shirt. "My father. Ollie. He almost killed you, and Levi's in danger and now I'm pregnant. Are we going to let him take them away, too?"

She let his shirt go when he didn't answer and walked towards the door. Levi quickly ducked away.

"He's not after Levi. He doesn't have the mark."

Her footsteps stopped.

"Cerva is mad *at us. Don't you understand? I renounced my faith and called it a curse," she said. "So lays upon this a curse of the prey. Neither of my babies are safe. I'm going to kill him."*

"Is that what you're going to tell our kids, Charlotte? That you killed someone to keep them safe? How are they going to take that?"

Levi shook his head. He just wanted the bad man gone. He didn't care if his mom had to kill him to do it. What if he killed her first? Or his baby sibling in her belly?

"Dammit." His mother slammed her fist into the wall Levi was hiding behind. He could hear it crumble on the other side. "I..."

"Sealing it away and making him spend the rest of his life powerless. Doesn't that sound better than killing someone?"

"Because," Levi said, sighing because he already knew what their rebuttal was going to be. "It can't be someone from the five tribes who seals it. It has to be a magicless outsider."

Just as he assumed, both Oliver and Kara's eyes went to Lynn, who looked back at both in shock.

"I-I..." Lynn struggled to find her voice. "Well, I don't have magic. I could seal it."

"I don't think so," Levi said. "I'm not dragging a powerless inconvenience in front of Eric. You know why? Because he'll kill you without even batting an eye."

Levi knew if they had to drag her helpless self around with them, it'd end up just like with his dad. She'd manage to get in the way somehow, ruin things, and eventually end up making someone do something stupid to save her.

"B-But how else are we going to-"

"Exactly like I said, Ollie. We're going to kill him, yeah?"

Even though he was offering solid evidence against sealing his power, no one seemed convinced.

"I-I just don't think I can kill someone." Oliver's eyes went to the ground. "And I don't think this is what Mom would've wanted."

Levi had to use every amount of strength in his body to keep his mouth from falling open. His little brother had no idea. He thought their mom had been a pacifist. His image of her was entirely skewed, pure, and raw. Levi found himself biting his tongue to fight back the urge to sully it.

"Well, Mom would…" He couldn't do this to Oliver. "She…"

Oliver's eyes were on him, staring and waiting for Levi to fill in the blanks of his past he'd either forgotten or had been shielded from. He was waiting for Levi to tell him how great and proud and sweet their mother was.

And she was all those things…he could remember her content whistling as she cleaned the house, her prideful tone as she used to tell him stories of her tribe, and her blatant courage anytime they ran into a threat…but more than all of that, he remembered her hate for Eric. She wanted him as dead as their family was.

Could Oliver really have forgotten? Or was it that he didn't know her as well as Levi did?

"No…I guess you're right. She wouldn't want this."

Oh, why was he doing this? He knew full well that saying it meant they were going to go with the plan of sealing Eric's power. He was ignoring the blinking red signs in his head reminding him that even killing Eric would be next to impossible. Now Levi was going to try to injure him enough for this vulnerable girl to get up and rid him of his powers?

Levi. Levi, Levi, Levi. Come on. You know you've got this. You've got your thunder spell, dude.

He rolled his eyes. Yeah, he did have it, but he still hadn't mastered it yet.

Mastered. You're close enough.

Plus, the spell wasn't made for mortal, non-gods. His body wasn't capable of using it without it injuring him. Sometimes severely.

His eyes went to the burns on his fingers. This was on the less severe side, but it still hurt like crap.

Fair point. But it's whatever.

Whatever?

Whatever.

He shrugged his shoulders. That worked for him. As much as anything else did, anyway.

"Levi?" Oliver asked. "What are you doing?"

Levi's eyes came back into focus as he remembered that they were all having a conversation.

"Oh, he's just talking to the alter ego in his head." Kara smirked. "He does that a lot."

"What?" Levi asked. "What? No, I was just thinking."

So, contrary to usual, he was going to have to plan this one out. There were too many other factors beside himself. If it was just him, he'd go with his instincts. But now he had people who had no magic, his little brother, and even though Kara could theoretically protect herself, he didn't trust that Eric wouldn't think of her as an easy target.

"Okay. We'll seal his powers away," Levi said. "But that's going require two things. One, we're going to have to teach *her* how to do the sealing ritual. Two, we're going to have to teach you something other than parlor tricks, Ollie."

"You…you're going to teach me more magic?" Oliver's face lit up the exact same way as when they were little. Levi gave him an enthusiastic nod. "Okay!"

Lynn shook her head.

"But what if I can't do it?" She stared down at her hands. "What if I can't do the seal?"

"Oh, no, none of that self-doubting bullshit," Levi said. "You got blood, don't you?"

"Y-Yeah."

"Then you can do the seal."

Levi watched Oliver's hand wrap around hers as he gave her a smile. He felt bad for being so harsh, but this was, as he told Oliver before, life or death. If even one person was unsure or hesitated, it was all over.

"You can do it," Oliver whispered. "We're going to get through this, Lynn, remember?"

She nodded as she took in a deep breath.

"Okay. We need to save Dad," she said. "Show me how to do the seal."

"Now that's more like it." Levi's mouth twisted into a grin. "Come with me."

They needed to act fast and secretly. If Eric knew the two of them were together and out in the open, he would come after them fast. It didn't matter if he was in pain.

But like always, Levi had a solution for that.

***

"Are you sure this is where you want out? There's…nothing here."

Levi stared at the taxi driver. It didn't take a genius to know what he was thinking. Most of the time when taxi drivers left someone somewhere like this – a large field way on the outskirts of town – murder was involved. That was unfortunately not the case.

"Yeah," Levi said. "Thanks. Here's two hundred. Keep the change."

The taxi driver raised his eyebrows, shrugged, and sped off when Levi closed the door.

As they made their way farther into the open field, Levi felt the tall, sturdy grass rub against his pant leg. He'd looked up a map of this place on his phone, and it looked exactly the same in person. It was entirely bare of anything other than small, shrub-like trees, and he couldn't see a house anywhere. The only thing that obstructed his view was a forest in the distance. And as he held his breath to listen, he couldn't hear anything besides the occasional bird, and small, scurrying ahead of them. It had him wondering what kind of birds and animals were bustling around that were too fast for him to catch a glimpse of.

Levi noticed that an ominous, yet strange silence had followed them from the taxi, but he couldn't understand why. *This* was the least terrifying part.

No scary parts for you, though.

Right. Levi was the furthest thing from scared.

He'd given it some thought on the long drive over and decided that he was actually okay with what they were going to do to Eric. The torture of losing his magic and being helpless would suit the damn Lupus. Maybe when Oliver turned his back, he would kick the asshole a couple of times, too.

"So." Lynn broke the silence. "Why do we have to come all the way out here?"

"The magic I'm going to teach Ollie is a little, well…" Levi paused. "Flashy. We need the room."

"What about Lynn's sealing thing?" Oliver asked. "Are you going to show her that first?"

The more Levi thought about the seal and the way blood was used to make it, the more his stomach began to sour.

"Uh, well," Levi said. "I'm going to show her the first time and Kara's going to work on it with her."

Kara nodded, and Levi sighed in relief. He was so glad Kara was here. As much as he hated to admit it, if she hadn't continued to pal around with him even after he left her the first time, he probably wouldn't be alive today. She was always the bridge between his impulsiveness and his logic.

"Okay, so here's what you do, yeah?" He pulled out his pocket knife. "You just…"

There was a lump in his throat, and he couldn't swallow it down for the life of him. His forehead was already covered in beads of sweat, and his hands were the same, if not worse. He was scared he was going to drop the knife if he didn't hurry.

"So Eric has a mark similar to mine and Ollie's." Levi dragged the knife across his five fingers. He then grabbed Lynn's hand. "You need to either draw it exactly how it looks on any part of his body, or find his actual mark. After you've done that, you seal it by placing all five of your fingers around it."

On the top of her hand, he drew a spiral with one tail coming off the top. He then branched it off from the middle of the tail with another, and then added three branches to that one.

"Five tails," Lynn said as she stared down at it.

"One for our grandfather, our mom, me, Ollie, and Macie." Levi said. "Our dad wasn't a Cerva. He was like you."

After a second, he realized how rude that sounded. He didn't mean it like that. He just meant that she was normal. At one time he would've envied that. Maybe he still did.

Levi's breath stopped as something soft – he could barely even hear it – dripped to the ground.

"Levi?" Kara moved closer. "Hold on, I'll-"

His vision blurred, and everything went black for a second, but as soon as Oliver caught him, it was all back in focus.

"Dammit," Levi growled, and his eyes met his blood on the ground. His vision blurred again. "Kara?"

"I got you."

A cool, tingling sensation started in his fingertips, and he felt his energy return to him. With the support of his brother, he was once again on his feet.

"Sorry about that," Levi mumbled. "Anyway. One more thing before we begin."

He fished in his pocket, hoping he hadn't lost it on the trip over here. His hand eventually closed around a pen-shaped item.

"What's that?" Oliver asked. "And what's that mark on it?"

"Your brother has a bad habit of *borrowing* things from people without their knowledge," Kara said, her eyes rolling when Levi grinned. "That's the mark of the Vulpes. Some say they're more vicious than the Lupus. Which is why I'm somewhat surprised that you have that, Levi."

Levi stared down at it, first fondly, then with a shiver. Carved into the metal coating was, of course, a spiral, but it was upside down, contrary to the marks of the other tribes. The tails coming off the end, in this case two of them, were curvy and long. Almost snake-like.

"Oh, you know who I got it from," Levi said, but Kara gave him a funny look. "Uh, Zoe had me hold onto it. You know, before she tried to kill me."

As expected, Kara's facial expression scrunched up. She'd always been jealous of Zoe. Even though Zoe tried to kill him, and he had zero interest in her after that.

"Zoe?" Oliver wrinkled his nose. "Who?"

"She was one of the first people I met when I left home." Levi tried to look as if he didn't care. "She was a Vulpes I met in Australia when I was a forest ranger. That's all."

If Kara rolled her eyes much more, they were going to fall out of her head.

"Anyway, the Vulpes use necromancy," he said, sticking the pen in the ground. "As in, all the dead people stuff. But when you play with the dead, you don't want them to go do their own thing, so this thing makes an invisible forcefield to keep magic in."

It covered a large area, too. Meaning no matter what magic they used, it would be untraceable.

"I'll take Lynn over here so you don't faint again," Kara said. "Come on, Lynn."

"O-Okay."

He was going to hear about this later.

As Levi turned to his little brother, he noticed his gaze lingering in Lynn's direction, following her every step. He was so infatuated with her that he probably didn't have a clue. Levi knew that feeling well, as he unfortunately was known for wearing his heart on his sleeve.

"I guess you do love her, huh?" Levi asked, and Oliver turned. "Well?"

"Love her?" Oliver's eyes were wide. "Oh, um, I don't know. I guess I haven't really thought about it."

Levi's laugh was loud as it filled the empty air around them. He wished he was as oblivious to his feelings as his little brother was. Maybe it wouldn't have been so hard to leave America the first time he came over. But, again, he felt responsible and hypersensitive to everything. Especially love.

"Haven't thought about it? You hold hands, you stare at her...but what do I know?" Levi shrugged. "Anyway, we have to use our time wisely. This thing doesn't last forever."

"Right," Oliver said slowly. "So, what are we gonna learn?"

Levi pulled his jacket off, freeing his arms and shoulders. He knew his brother wouldn't be able to use the same thunder spell that he could. Not only was it god magic, but it was the highest class. Plus, Oliver was never good with electrical magic. When he brought home a battery that one time, Oliver couldn't even make anything happen with it.

But his fire magic...

"Well, there's only one way to beat Eric, and that's using magic beyond the level he can use. For example, I have this thunder spell that nearly wipes me off the face of the earth," Levi said. "But it almost wipes him out, too."

"Are you going to show me that?" Before Levi could start to say no, Oliver's hands clapped together. "Please, please. I-I can do it. Just show me and I'll do it."

Again, this was just like when they were younger. He could never say no to his little brother. Especially when Oliver was so eager to learn. Who knew, maybe he *could* use the thunder magic.

"Hold on," Levi said. "Let's work up to it first. Let me show you a different trick that's just a little easier."

"Okay, I'm ready."

Levi cracked his neck to one side, and then the other. Energy was coursing through his veins, and as he concentrated on the soles of his feet, a warm sensation spread through the ground. He held out his hand, forcing the energy to shoot back up to his fingertips.

"Fire."

The ground shook as the spot in front of him began to split open. He yanked his arm backwards, and the fire exploded from the crack.

Oliver watched it, speechless, and Levi couldn't help but smile. After all these years, his little brother was still impressed by his magic. But, he had to say, he was also pretty blown away by his own control. Before, he wasn't even able to cast anything more than a small fireball.

"After you learn how to do that, you can pull it from the ground and control its path," he said. "If you can master that, I'll teach you the thunder one, yeah?"

"Yeah!" Oliver nodded. "Okay, so I just say the spell and-"

"Whoa, whoa! No!" Levi said quickly. "You have to concentrate all your energy in the soles of your feet first. Be careful. This spell's a little crazy."

If Oliver were to just try to summon up this kind of power incorrectly, he could seriously hurt himself. Levi knew that all too well.

"I think it's working!" Oliver said. Levi could feel the ground getting warmer. "Now I'll put my hand forward and-"

The ground violently split open in front of them, and the fire came blasting out uncontrollably.

"Dammit." Levi held out his hand. "Stop!"

The fire that was starting to rain down upon them came to a halt just inches above their heads.

Oliver slowly looked up, his eyes widening as he stared at the fire.

"Uh. Oops."

"Oops is right," Levi said. "I told you, be careful, buddy."

Oliver looked down at his hands as Levi sighed. Honestly, that was way better than *his* first time casting the spell, but this wasn't going to do. They needed to get rid of Eric within the next day if they wanted the upper hand. He'd have to perfect his thunder spell now.

"No, but that was really good. I can tell you've been practicing your control." Levi smiled when Oliver's face lit up. "Since you did so much better than I did the first time, let me show you the really hard one. Just to see, not to do, though."

He planted his feet firmly on the ground.

He could do this.

Last time, when he was holding Eric off, he knew what mistake he'd made. The thunder came at him and he reacted too quickly in fear that Eric would attack him before he was done. If he waited and took his time, he'd have it down.

Yeah, see? Basically perfected.

Levi watched as the dark clouds made their appearance in the sky, dimming the lighting around them and stacking on top of one another.

"Uh, Levi?" Kara called. "Are you sure you want to do that now?"

Distant lightning in front of him, deep rumbles from the clouds… This was it. He had to get it right this time so he could do it again later.

"Thunder."

The sky flashed, and everything transitioned into slow motion. As Levi looked up, the bolt was already above his head. He reached up and felt the electricity surge painfully through his body, lighting up every organ and muscle. His mind was racing with a million thoughts and wouldn't slow down no matter how hard he tried.

Okay, now throw it at the tree-

As he let go, it… slipped, if that was even possible, and his hand felt like it was on fire as the lightning flew into the tree.

A shrill ringing noise rang in his eardrums as he watched the tree split in half and absorb the shock. Branches flew every direction, some nearly sparking to life,

"Levi?"

He couldn't breathe.

Had he done something stupid? Where was the air? His eyes went to his brother's, who appeared to be breathing just fine.

Wait, his brother's mouth was moving, too, but he couldn't hear anything other than the painful ringing that was getting louder and louder. His arm had lost feeling and was spasming out of control. The air was still gone. Where was-

"Levi?"

The sound, air, and the feeling in his arm all returned at once. It was almost too much with the pressure building in his head.

"A-Are you okay?" Oliver grabbed him by the shoulders. "Hey?"

"Uh." Levi had to physically stop himself from gasping. "Yeah. No, I'm fine. What'd you think?"

Oliver turned and stared at the tree just as one side of it collapsed to the ground.

"That was…wow," he said. "If I try that-"

"No way," Levi said. "Not yet. After we're done with Eric, you can try it then, yeah?"

His voice came out more rushed than he meant it to. What was up with him right now?

"Y-Yeah."

"Come on, we should head home." Levi turned towards Kara. "Kara, Lynn, let's go."

As they all hurried behind him, and he dialed his phone to call a cab, his mind raced. That was the worst thunder magic he'd cast since he first learned how to use magic altogether. His eyes went down to the new burn marks that littered his hand, but this time there was one that had streaked up his forearm.

Eric was right. He was falling apart, slowly losing his touch the more anxious he got.

And now he was going to attempt to do something that not even his mother, one of the most powerful Cervas in history, could do. He was crazy.

Stupid.

He was going to get them all killed just because he wanted to keep his little brother happy.

He was a damn idiot.

Chapter 8

"Night, buddy. Don't stay up too late."

Oliver watched as Levi and Kara disappeared into the other room, leaving him and Lynn alone for the first time since before he jumped. He was almost relieved. Even though he loved his brother's company, he needed time to process things.

More importantly, he needed to talk to Lynn. He needed to explain himself, and he also had to ask if this was all too much for her. The look on her face when Levi showed her the seal was the same one she'd had on the rooftop. Pure terror.

"Um, so Lynn, are-"

A pillow slammed into Oliver's face before he could finish, almost knocking him off the bed. When he recovered, Lynn was glaring at him, her thick eyebrows slanted so drastically they could stab someone through.

"How dare you?" she finally forced out. Her face was a deep shade of red.

"H-How dare I? Um-"

"How could you jump like that? How could you run from me?" she asked. Her sentences were running together the angrier she got. "I thought we were in this together. You just took it all upon yourself to handle things, didn't you? Well, what about me, huh? Did you ever consider how this was going to affect me?"

Oliver's mouth was almost to the ground as he realized they hadn't talked about what happened in that moment yet. He still hadn't explained to her why he did what he did.

"I'm sorry, Lynn, I guess I wasn't think-"

"I guess you weren't!" She growled, throwing another pillow at him. This time he stopped it midair with just a look. "No, you don't get to do that!"

She climbed onto the bed, yanked the pillow out of the air, and started hitting him with it. Oliver didn't stop her this time, though. He just let her continue to swing the pillow at his head and his body. It didn't hurt, after all.

"You. Stupid. Idiot." She hit him with each word. "I almost lost you! You were going to leave me!"

Between hits, which were now getting quite a bit harder, he saw tears beginning to roll down her face.

"I was so scared," she continued. "He tried to put me to sleep but I could still see you shove yourself off. Your body went limp and you started to fall and there wasn't anything I could do!"

"Lynn-"

"You asshole!" She hit him harder. "How could you give up like that? I thought I was important to you!"

"Lynn, come on." Oliver grabbed her wrists, and the pillow flew from her hand, but she continued to try and swing at him. "Lynn."

Her struggling eventually weakened into sobs as he held her in place by her wrists.

"H-How could you...you stupid..."

"If I let go of your wrists, are you going to try to punch me?" Oliver asked softly. She mumbled out a yes, making him sigh. "No, you're not. Come here."

The moment he freed her and pulled her against his chest, he could feel her pain rip through his body. Even as he hugged her as tight as he could, trying to reassure her everything was okay, she still cried, her fingers winding themselves into his shirt.

He had no idea what to say. Talking and calming people down wasn't his strong suit. He'd only learned how to calm himself down kind of from all his time on the ship. It was a necessity because of all of how chaotic Mr. Bain made his life. He was constantly on edge and made sure he did everything entirely perfect because Mr. Bain didn't forgive. But honestly, what was he *supposed* to say? How could he tell her he wasn't really thinking about anything right before he jumped? Her possibly being sad or angry with him didn't occur to him. He was *killing* himself. Everything would have been a distant memory before he hit the bottom.

"Lynn?" he asked. "Hey, look at me."

He pulled her away from his chest so he could see her face.

Her makeup was smeared from where she'd rubbed her cheek into his shirt, and her brown eyes were vibrant against the puffy red skin around them. She stared at him, her soft lower lip poking out and trembling ever so slightly.

Even though she looked like an absolute mess in every way, worn out, worried, and overwhelmed with emotion, she'd never been more beautiful. He couldn't get rid of the butterflies racing from his stomach and up through his chest.

He placed his hands on either side of her face, her shallow breathing becoming more apparent against his warm skin.

"I-"

Lynn's lips smashed against his before he could say anything else, and as he sat there stunned, she wrapped her arms around him, pulling their bodies closer to one another. Her lips were like velvet, and her body – his hands traced the figure of her sides and hips – fit perfectly against his as she straddled his waist to get even closer. Her fingers tangled into his hair so she could kiss him fiercer and more passionately. He didn't have time to breathe before she pulled him back against her eager lips for more again and again.

She gave him a moment to catch his breath as she stared at him, her expression one he wasn't familiar with. But it wasn't long before she shoved him down by his chest and continued to *attack* him with her greedy, lustful lips. Her hand mirrored what his had done moments ago, tracing his chest, his sides, his hips… stopping right on the meaty part of his leg. His heart was racing as he panted, wondering whether or not he should stop her. But his thoughts were becoming cloudy as her nails dug into this shoulder and her hips pressed against his.

"L-Lynn," Oliver broke their lips apart. "Lynn, is this something you want to…"

Her eyes looked like they'd come back into focus as she gasped for air, the same as him.

Neither of them said anything, but her large brown eyes held his gaze. He couldn't look away as they watched one another try to regulate their breathing.

Finally, when Oliver thought he could finally form a full sentence, he cleared his throat.

"W-Well, that was nice," he breathed out. "And unexpected. I thought you were mad at me."

The air around them was tense as her expression still dripped with lust.

"I am," she whispered. "I'm just…"

Her warm breath punched his skin as her mouth hung open slightly and she struggled to find her words. Her eyebrows pressed together, and she shook her head softly.

"Y-You don't have to say anything else," Oliver whispered. His insides clenched as he noticed the body heat radiating from her hips. "I'm sorry, Lynn. I-I really am. I shouldn't have done that to you and I was wrong to-"

"It's okay." Her face was inches from his again. "I'm sorry for hitting you with the pillow."

"No, I…" Her lips rubbed against his. "It didn't…hurt."

Her fingers tightened in his hair once more, but her kisses were soft this time. Light and playful before she pulled back to give him a long, hard look.

"Oliver, I…" Her hand squeezed his outer thigh. "Do you think we…"

She was vulnerable right now. She was upset, flustered, tired… Oliver knew exactly what she was going to say. Something inside of him was trying to get him to give in and agree, but something else told him that if he did, he might ruin their relationship forever. He couldn't take advantage of her like this.

"I think we should go to bed," he whispered, brushing her hair behind her ear. "We've both had a long day."

Lynn didn't say anything, but she didn't have to. The disappointment in her eyes, but also the relief, said it all. He was disappointed, too, but this was for the best, he was sure. There was nothing he'd love more than to let her do as she wished and allow her hands to do what they'd set out to do when she first started kissing him, but it couldn't be now. It had to be under different terms when they were both stable and ready to make a commitment like this to one another. He didn't want their first time together to be one she remembered regretfully.

"Okay," she finally said. Her body began to lift off his. "I should get the light…"

"I got it." Oliver narrowed his eyes, and the switch clicked off. "You can, um, keep lying here. I-If you want."

Her cheek pressed against his chest as she lay back down on him.

"Goodnight, Oliver."

He held her tightly between his arms, her breathing becoming rhythmic after a few short minutes. He couldn't help but sigh in relief, but also contentment.

With all the crap going on right now, it was just nice to be close to someone he really, truly cared about.

***

The sound of running water woke Oliver slowly. His head was almost pounding as he turned on his side so he could squint towards the bright, barely cracked window to see if it was raining.

It wasn't, so he rolled back over and pressed his face into the soft pillow. He was so cold right now, which was a huge difference from how he'd felt last night. He was so warm that he was sweating worse than if he'd gone for a run. Lynn was so-

His body shot up as he noticed Lynn wasn't in bed with him. He scanned the room, relieved to see her things still in the same spots they were last night. But where could she be?

"Um, Oliver?"

He turned back towards the window to see Lynn standing in the bathroom doorway, a towel wrapped around her body, catching the drips from her sopping wet hair.

"O-Oh! Hey," he said, his face heating. "What are you, um, doing?"

"Well, I didn't want to drip water on the carpet." Her face was as red as his felt as she stared at her feet. "I was wondering if you could grab my clothes for me?"

For a second, nothing she said processed in his head. But when she gazed up at him, her autumn eyes warming his body enough to think, he got up and gathered her clothes.

"Here," he said. Her eyes didn't leave his as she took them softly from his hand. "Are you okay?"

"I, well," she struggled. "I'm…sorry about last night."

"No, it's okay. It doesn't hurt when you get hit with a pillow, you know."

She gasped as he placed his hand against her cheek. It was warm and wet from her shower, which heated his ice-cold fingers. He rubbed his thumb across it, catching water droplets from her forehead.

"I-I meant…about the other thing," she said. "The kissing thing."

"Oh." Oliver's hand immediately dropped from her face. "Oh. Well, I'm not."

Why did she seem so uncomfortable? Just last night she had her body pressed against his and was ready to…do other things with him. Was it because he didn't do the last thing she wanted?

"I was angry and confused and I-"

"I think you're really great, Lynn," Oliver said. "I mean that."

"I think you're really great too, but-"

"But what?"

Lynn shook her head as she backed into the bathroom and closed the door.

But what?

If they both thought highly of one another, what else was there? He didn't understand.

Oliver made his way back over to the bed and collapsed onto it. It felt like he couldn't do anything right these past couple of days. He almost didn't escape from Eric, he couldn't use the fire spell his brother had tried to teach him, and he couldn't…well, he didn't know what was up with Lynn, but he wasn't doing something right for her. She'd surprised him when she kissed him last night, so doing anything else in that moment wasn't an option, but maybe he should've stopped her after he regained his composure.

"We just can't…" Oliver sat back up when he heard Lynn's voice. "I'm a mess, Oliver."

She was standing in the doorway again, her clothes sloppily hanging on her body, her hair still soaked.

"What?"

"You deserve better than me," she said. "You shouldn't have to put up with my mess of a life."

Oliver tilted his head at her.

"I don't understand?"

"It's been almost three weeks, Oliver." She threaded her fingers in her hair. "It's been three weeks and I still have these cravings. I-I'm bound to relapse soon, and you don't deserve to have to deal with the craziness of-"

"Lynn…have you been listening to what's been going on in *my* life?" Oliver almost laughed. "Mine's not too easy either. If anything, you're the one who doesn't deserve to have to put up with my problems."

She kept staring at him, her eyes searching for an answer. But there was something else wrong that she wasn't telling him. He didn't know what, but he could just tell.

"Are you going to leave after this?" Lynn asked quietly. "After we save my dad?"

"Not…if you don't want me to," he said. "Do you want me to?"

Her eyebrows pushed together, and she shook her head quickly.

"N-No, I want you to stay," she said. "I don't think, well, I don't think I could live without you, Oliver."

She slowly made her way over to him and sat on the bed, never once breaking eye contact. Their faces were inches apart, and once again the intense heat between their bodies flared up. Her eyes pleaded and begged him for something as she reached forward and wrapped her hand around his. Her lips tempted him with memories from last night of their soft but feral assault on him.

He pressed his lips against hers, and they welcomed him with hunger. Soon they were both in the same position as last night, but this time *she* was underneath him. But that didn't mean she let him take any kind of control. She still guided him with knowledgeable-

"Ollie, Lynn, can you come in here for a sec?"

They both froze at Levi's voice in the other room. Oliver had nearly forgotten that there were other people here besides the two of them, and he was almost disappointed at the realization.

Neither of them said anything, but it wasn't from a lack of trying. Oliver was totally *entranced* by the way Lynn's eyes devoured the very image of him, and he was also surprised by his body's avidity at the thought of continuing to do whatever she wanted of him.

"Ollie?"

"Uh, y-yeah," Oliver forced out. "Just a sec."

Oliver reluctantly lifted himself from the bed and held out his hand. Lynn took it hesitantly and she followed behind him to see both Kara and Levi staring at the television. Levi's arms were crossed, and Kara's hand went to her forehead.

"Hey, what's the matter-"

"Reports say that upcoming star magician Oliver Lee has gone missing, and his apartment is empty," the girl on the TV said. "Oliver's partner and manager, magician Nik Rafiel, was interviewed late last night."

"Normally he returns my calls. I can't help but think someone's behind this," Nik said, standing in front of Oliver's apartment. "He was in a good apartment building, but everyone knew where he lived, so it's likely someone might've kidnapped him."

Oliver rolled his eyes. Nik's hair was tousled, and his clothes looked like they'd just been in a fight with a bear or something. They were wrinkled, half unbuttoned, and there was even a stain on his yellow tie. And his face. A lot of people didn't believe Nik when he'd causally mention in interviews that he was an insomniac, but if there was ever a time to believe it, it was now. There were purple bags under his eyes, five o'clock shadow on half of his face, and he had that twisted mouth expression that screamed conspiracy theorist. That was just like Nik to be so paranoid. If everyone else around him didn't look so serious, he would've laughed.

"Police are saying this is a valid suspicion," the girl said. "They say when they went to the apartment where Oliver resided, the main door was smashed in, and the lock on Oliver's personal room looked to have been tampered with."

"I saw the little boy running," a woman he recognized from his apartment said. "A couple minutes after, this African American fellow came casually strolling out. I didn't recognize him."

Levi turned the TV off and sighed.

"Ollie, did you *have* to become famous?" he asked. "Laying low would've been a better option, buddy. Don't you think advertising yourself like that was a little silly?"

Oliver shrugged his shoulders as he looked down at the ground.

"Oops."

"Apparently the police are everywhere looking for you," Levi said. "We need make this quick."

Everyone looked up at Levi with wide eyes.

"Surely we have a little more time," Kara said. "Oliver still hasn't mastered-"

"There's no more time. He'll be able to do it in the heat of the moment. That's how it always works," Levi said. "But more importantly, are you ready, Lynn?"

"Uh…huh."

Oliver wasn't sure whether or not she was still in a daze from what had happened in the room, or if deep down she was frightened. Maybe it was both.

Levi shook his head.

"No, I need you to really be ready, yeah? If you mess up, it's over."

"Yeah, no, I'm ready." Lynn nodded, her fingers wrapping around each other tight enough to turn them red.

"Good, then let's-"

Oliver's breathing stopped as a sharp pain ripped through his head, sending him stumbling backwards into the dresser.

"Oliver?"

"Dammit. Kara, I need you to-"

Oliver's eyes fluttered open, and he was met with the familiar, bright wooden walls of the cruise ship. He expected, as he looked down at his hands, for them to be someone else's, because that was always how these strange visions worked, but they weren't. They were his hands, the same ones he'd had two seconds before the headache-

"Idiot."

Oliver's ears perked as the air around him suddenly became nostalgic. Where had he seen this?

He walked forward around the small, closed off room, trying desperately to remember. Only when the door was unlocked and opened to reveal both James and Mr. Bain did he remember what exactly was happening.

"No..." Oliver backed away. "No, no, please."

"James, do as I told you."

Oliver tried to back away fast enough, but James had already grabbed him by his neck.

"F-Fire."

His magic did nothing as he was slammed to the ground on his stomach, and his hands were tied tightly behind his back.

"On this cruise ship you'll do as you're instructed without question, boy," Mr. Bain said. As soon as he snapped his fingers, Oliver felt something sharp rip through his right upper arm. "You will not use your magic."

Another slice, this time on his other arm.

"S-Stop," Oliver struggled to say. He was rewarded this time with a stab in his shoulder. "Please!"

James continued to carve and puncture his arms until Mr. Bain cleared his throat.

"You'll do as I say, boy. Do you understand?"

"Y-Yes..."

He snapped his fingers again, and James did the same thing to his back as he did to his arms. Oliver cried out with each new wound, but neither of them seemed affected in any way.

"Yes what?"

"Yes, s-sir..." Oliver could feel the blood oozing down his body. "P-Please, sir."

Mr. Bain's laugh made Oliver cringe.

"Remember this the next time you think about crossing me," he said. "Come on, James."

The large man rose to his feet but lingered over Oliver's body for a second.

"Sir, shouldn't we get a medic to clean him-"

"We'll let him bleed out for a bit before we do that. Come."

The door shut, and the lights went off, leaving him alone as he tried his best to hold in his tears. He didn't know why he was holding back. He could see that the light underneath the door was free from anyone's feet, meaning that the only person he was trying to prove he was strong to was himself.

As he lay there, squeezing his eyes shut so they wouldn't send any more liquid from his body, he started to hear a ringing noise. His body felt cold and his heart was beating heavy against his eardrums, competing with the shrill pitch in his ears to be heard. The black corners of the room started to lose their pigment on the edges, turning white and-

Oliver's lungs inflated with air as a tingly sensation brought him back to the present. He shoved off whatever was pinning him to the bed and sat up, scooting back against the bed frame. Energy was gathering in his palms, and he readied himself to-

"Ollie, buddy!" Levi's face came into view through his tunnel vision. "It's okay!"

As his line of sight expanded back to normal, Oliver realized he was in the hotel room with everyone. His mouth tried to form words, but his brain refused to talk to him.

"I...the ship..." Oliver struggled to say. "He..."

He ripped his long-sleeved shirt off so he could stare at his arms. They were smooth and dry; the only remnants of his horrible memory were the discolored scars littered across his skin.

"That asshole," Levi growled. "We need to end this."

"Levi, your brother's in no condition to-"

Oliver watched as his brother's eyes grew wide, and he grabbed his head with both hands.

"Dammit, dammit. Now he's doing it to me," he said. "Kara, the pen in my p-ocket. Use i-it now."

Kara rushed over to Levi's jacket just as another pain spiked through Oliver's head. He tried to resist it as best as he could, but he found himself blacking out and waking up in another memory.

Chapter 9

This was getting old and annoying. The damn coward needed to come after them and challenge them head on. Levi wondered if this irritation was the same thing Eric felt every time Levi slipped through his fingertips.

"Levi!"

Color drained from Levi's face as the knife hurtled past his head and into the wooden pole to which he was tied. It was so close to him that he could feel the cold metal against the tip of his ear.

"Let him go! Stop!" Kara cried. "Levi!"

Was he...in New Zealand?

His gaze followed the line of Lupus in front of him. They were in a small, run-down village, and Kara... he turned his head and followed the sound of her shrieking to see her in a cage made up of thick tree branches. Her arms were bound behind her and she was guarded by two larger men. It almost looked like they were in the old Cerva village, but as another knife fell past him, nicking his other ear, he recognized the memory. This was when he and Kara were trying to draw Eric off Oliver's trail, but there was only one problem... Eric wasn't here during this moment. So...

How was he able to recreate it in Levi's mind?

"Theve, you're getting awful close to hitting him," one of the Lupus said with a laugh. "Eric's not going to like if his precious prize is damaged."

"Oh, he won't mind if I rough him up," Theve said. Another knife flew past Levi's head. "You got a smart mouth on you, don't you little Cerva boy?"

Levi glared at him as they all cackled wildly.

"Girl, you're lucky you're a Silvan. Otherwise we'd have plans for you," a different Lupus said.

"Don't you dare touch her," Levi growled. "I'll kill each and every one of you."

He felt blood beginning to trickle down his ear and face as everything in front of him began to blur.

"Yeah, I'd like to see you-"

The group of Lupus began to part, and Levi's eyes zeroed in on Eric as he walked between them.

"This…this isn't even remotely how this happened." Levi shook his head. "How are you fabricating memories for me?"

His eyes widened as he saw three people tied to ropes dragging behind him. When Eric moved out of the way, Oliver, their mother, and Macie all looked up at him with pleading eyes. Their mouths were taped shut, and their hands were tied together, but his mother continued to struggle.

"What a nice family reunion," Eric said. "You're all together."

"This isn't how this happened. What are you going to-" Levi's voice choked as Eric pulled out his knife and grabbed Oliver by his hair. "Eric, no, don't do this to me. Don't be a coward like this."

The knife pierced through his little brother's chest, making their mother cry out as much as she could through the tape over her mouth. The crowd of Lupus, which looked to have gained size, laughed in response.

"Coward?" Eric moved over to Macie, also grabbing her by the hair. His knife danced lightly against her throat. "Does this make me a coward?"

Levi had to close his eyes as his sister's blood spewed across his face. When her body thudded to the ground, he reopened them to see Eric standing behind his mother.

"No, please, Eric. I'll beg, okay?" Levi said. "I'll do anything. Don't...don't kill her."

Levi knew this was a memory, and he knew his mother was already dead...but he couldn't see it again. She was everything to him.

Eric stopped, tilted his head, and cracked a smile.

"Beg, you say?" he asked. "I'll hear it."

Levi bit the inside of his cheek.

"E-Eric, please. Don't kill her, yeah? Getting celebrated after you die because you completely wiped out a bloodline is pretty bullshit," Levi said. "It won't happen, and she doesn't deserve to die. Please, just kill me, and then you can let her go."

"That wasn't very good."

"Okay, let me try again-"

The knife stabbed through his mother's chest as tears poured from her eyes like waterfalls.

"Mom!" Levi screamed. He struggled to free himself from the binds. "I swear I'm going to kill you, you fucking coward."

Eric laughed as he walked towards Levi. He wiped the blood from his knife on his pant leg, readying it for its next victim.

"Do it!" Levi struggled more. "I dare you! Do it, Eric!"

Eric pulled back the knife, and Levi could see the gleam in his eyes.

"Thunder!"

Levi knew the exact moment he came to, because his hand collided against something metal, sending a surge of pain through his knuckles.

"Shit." He yanked his hand back and held it tightly. His mind immediately went to his brother. "Is Ollie okay? Where is he?"

Levi was fine, to say in the least. He'd gone through memory after memory with Eric. He was used to it, but his brother wasn't. What he couldn't figure out, though, was how Eric twisted his memories this much. He must've heard about what happened from his tribe and then recreated it almost exactly. Exactly plus two people whc didn't exist anymore and one who was on the other side of the world. That wasn't an ability he knew about at all.

"He's fine, Levi," Kara sighed. "He's out on the balcony. He had to get some fresh air."

Levi studied Kara's expression closely. It was tightened and paler than usual, and he could tell she was biting the inside of her cheek to hold something back.

"What...did Eric show him?" Levi asked slowly. "Kara?"

She closed her eyes and took in a deep breath, composing herself before she opened them back up.

"Your mother and sister."

Levi shook his head. He was surprised Eric hadn't already showed him that, but it appeared he was either grasping for straws to get them to come out, or he was still pissed from his and Levi's last showdown. Eric was normally restrained when it came to showing memories. He liked to stress his prey out so they'd panic and make a mistake. Or in Levi's case, get angry and come barreling after him like a mad man. Now he was using them as a means of direct attack.

"Lynn's out there with him. He's not taking it well," Kara said. "I tried to stop it as quickly as I could but…"

"It's alright, Kara. Thank you."

Levi made his way to the balcony to find Oliver leaning over the railing. Lynn was rubbing his back, whispering to him.

"Ollie," Levi said, and Lynn spun around. "Lynn, do you mind if we…"

Lynn nodded, patted Oliver on the back one last time, and shrugged her way around Levi, lingering only for a moment at the door.

Levi rested against the railing beside his brother, whose forehead was pressed against his clasped hands. He knew exactly how Oliver felt. Eric showed him that vision again and again and it never became any easier to watch. He thought after a while that he would become desensitized to it, but he found his already broken heart shattering into even tinier pieces each time.

"Hey, bud. You okay?"

"No, I…" Oliver paused. "I wanna kill him, Levi."

Levi was stunned. When his brother looked up at him, his eyes were stone cold and solemn.

"You don't, though," Levi sighed. "You're angry right now. If you were to do that you'd never forgive-"

"I want to kill him," Oliver said. "I can't believe I was going to let him live."

Levi wanted to kill him so much, too. But this wasn't his brother talking. It was the shock and fear and rage, something Levi had been living with for a long time. More recently the fear had taken front runner, as much as he hated to admit it.

He didn't want his brother to feel like he did. He didn't want him to have to live with the same shame as he did. It was all fun and games thinking about killing someone until you actually had to do it. He was ready to kill Eric in the beginning, but Levi knew *he* would've been the one to do it. He would've never let Oliver deliver the finishing blow.

"I'll be straight with you, buddy. Killing someone isn't as easy as it sounds," Levi said. "You might think it'll relieve some of the hurt, but it doesn't. At least, it never did for me."

"You've…"

"Mhm. There aren't too many things I've regretted doing in my life, you know. There are more things I regret *not* doing. But I *do* regret killing every person I have, regardless of my reasons."

Levi stared down at his hands as he remembered the throats he'd slit, the chests he'd stabbed, and every other way he'd fought for his survival. It was all necessary, he knew, otherwise he wouldn't be here today.

"Would you regret killing Mr. Bain?"

His eyes went to his brother's as a twinge of pain rode from the top of his head to his toes. He'd thought about this very thing for who knows how long now, and the sad part about it was that…

Maybe he actually would feel guilty and regretful about taking his sworn enemy's life. It didn't matter that Eric killed his mother and sister. Levi knew he'd be okay the moment he took Eric's life, but the look in someone's eyes as they died...the way they convulsed...

The feeling of an empty vessel when they were finally gone.

"I know *you* would."

It was silent, and Levi's chest burned from watching his brother. This kind of pain was something he was used to, but his brother wasn't accustomed to it.

"I just..." Oliver squeezed the railing. "I could've gone with them that day. I...I could've saved them."

"No, no, you couldn't have," Levi said. "It's like you said to me, bud. It's in the past now, and you didn't know it was going to happen. But we can save Lynn's dad. The...way mom would've wanted."

"Yeah." Oliver nodded. "Do you think we can do it?"

He wanted to say the honest, one-hundred percent true answer to his brother, but he found himself nodding instead. There was no sense in making him scared now, he guessed.

Eric's going down, Levi, and you know it.

He rolled his eyes. Sure, he knew it. That was why his stomach was knotted so tightly he felt like puking.

***

The car ride to the same spot as earlier felt even longer this time. He still had the Vulpes pen activated, meaning the presence of their magic wouldn't leak out, but his eyes still scanned the area constantly. When the cab driver came to a stop and gave him the standard strange look and dialogue about being let off in the middle of nowhere, Levi narrowed his eyes, and the driver shut up and drove away.

He could tell Oliver and Lynn wanted to ask how he did that, but the anxiety radiating from their bodies had them quiet and timid.

"Okay," Levi said, clicking the pen off. "Now, we wait. Eric'll find us. Always does."

As they waited, Lynn tapped her foot, Kara paced back and forth, and Oliver...where did Oliver go? He turned his head to find him a ways away, leaning against the scorched, blackened tree from earlier.

For a second, when he first glanced over, he looked like...

His mother stood with her arms crossed and head relaxed against a branch of the tree.

Levi shook his thoughts back to the present.

"Ollie, you okay?" Levi trotted over to him.

Oliver nodded as he turned to his brother.

"I was just thinking is all," he said. "What, um, what all did you do after you left home?"

The killing conversation earlier must have piqued his interest.

"Well, I did a lot. I was a park ranger in Australia. Wouldn't recommend," Levi said, grinning. "Lived with a German couple when I went to high school. College in Germany, then Russia. Joined a gang. Also wouldn't recommend."

"You joined a gang?"

"Yep." Levi took his jacket off and pulled his shirt down from his chest. "Tattooed and everything."

The star tattoo, on the same spot as Oliver's mark, brought back tons of old memories, all of which he shoved to the back of his mind. As much as he'd love to go back and visit all the chaotic, round-the-clock activities he'd participated in, he was tired of seeing visions of his past.

"What was that like?"

"Like I said, wouldn't recommend," Levi laughed. "That's one of those things I *don't* regret, though. I had a lot of great friends, a lot of great times."

He watched Oliver's expression as he processed everything Levi had said. One thing about Oliver was that he had a pretty good poker face, so it was hard to tell what he was thinking. At least that was the case when they were younger.

"I-I'm sorry," Oliver said, and Levi tilted his head. "I should've stopped you from leaving that day."

"Dad wouldn't have let me stay, Ollie," Levi said. "It wasn't your fault. Besides, I met some cool people and learned a lot. Again, something I don't regret."

"Yeah."

Levi glanced over at Kara and Lynn to make sure they were still okay. Kara had her hand on Lynn's back, whispering in her ear.

"Are you ready to take Eric down?" Levi asked. "After all these years?"

"I-I am. Mr. Bain has-"

"Don't call him *Mr. Bain,* Oliver," Levi interrupted. "You're giving him respect. Something he doesn't deserve."

Oliver's eyes crinkled, and he visibly *gulped.*

What had Eric done to him during his three years on the cruise ship?

"I...he..." Oliver stared down at his feet. "I'm ready to take him down."

That was good enough for Levi. Eventually Oliver would be able to drop the whole respectful title of his enemies. Ridding Eric of his powers would be the first step towards that. Once Oliver was more powerful than he was, it'd put things into a new perspective.

"He's sure taking a while to get here. I must've really done a number on him," Levi said. "Or he's a *coward* and is going to hide in the shadows thinking no one knows he's there."

Levi laughed when the field around them stayed silent and unmoving. The tall grass finally waved gently with the passing breeze, but it was the only thing that dared make a sound.

Oliver looked at him, forehead wrinkled.

"I think he's scared, and I think he knows that the two of us are going to be much more than he's used to handling," he continued. "Maybe he'd rather just sit back and bombard our thoughts with pesky, made up memories so he doesn't have to do the heavy lifting."

The whole time he and Oliver were talking, he'd had this strange feeling. The one where you'd swear you were being watched. While accustomed to this, especially in Russia when he was with his gang, he'd only felt it here in America when he knew Eric was following them. He wasn't a fool.

"Those are some interesting thoughts, rat." Eric stepped out from the tree line to their right. The way he moved from the shadows was almost nostalgic, reminiscent of the memory of their mother. "But the only people who should be scared are you two."

Levi heard Kara's and Lynn's slow and fearful footsteps behind them as he glared forward.

It was now or never. Everything he did now had to be accurate and well thought out. He risked losing his brother, the woman he loved, and even his own life.

He risked losing the battle he'd been fighting for the entirety of his existence.

Chapter 10

The thoughts in Oliver's head had gone silent as he stared into the eyes of his former captor. Something about him – the way he stood, the way his eyes commanded attention and obedience – made Oliver want to squeeze as tightly as he could into a corner somewhere. He never thought that he would be facing off against Mr. Bain like this. It was different from the last time; he'd intended to kill himself before Mr. Bain could. But this required strength and control.

This required him to be more powerful than the man who imprisoned him.

"We're not scared," Levi said. There wasn't even a shake in his voice. "But you should be."

Oliver wished he could be like his brother. Levi was fearless and determined. Why couldn't Oliver be like that?

"What about you, *boy?*" Eric's eyes went to Oliver. "Are you scared?"

The second Oliver paused felt like forever. All he could think about was the cruise ship. The countless beatings and conditioning, the other workers he'd watched Eric kill... then his mother and little sister. Eric was just as ruthless with them as he was with the workers, but that didn't make it any easier. Seeing him kill never got easier.

"N-No." Oliver was biting his tongue so hard he tasted blood. "I'm not."

"Well, that's a surprise." Mr. Bain pulled out a knife – the same one, Oliver noticed, that he'd had in the vision with his mother and sister. "After all this time, I guess you really are more like your mother-"

Before Mr. Bain could get anything else out, Levi's arm raised, and everything started in slow motion.

Out of the corner of his eye, Oliver saw the bright flash of fire burst from his brother's hand. The heat was almost too unbearable, and as Oliver took a step backwards, he bumped into something hard.

"Ollie-"

Mr. Bain's arm wrapped around Oliver's neck, choking him.

"Let me show you what happens when you interrupt me, you little rat." The sharp, gleaming knife came into Oliver's line of vision. "You're going to wish you let him fall from that building."

Oliver was disoriented as the knife came towards him, but someone was screaming. His ears perked as he listened hard. Whoever it was, they were screaming his name.

"Oliver!" Lynn's voice cut through the thickness of his thoughts. "Oliver, do something!"

His eyes widened and he whispered under his breath, sending the knife flying from Mr. Bain's hand and out into the grassy field.

"Fire," Oliver managed to say, his hand pointing directly at Mr Bain's head.

"Shit."

The grip released from around his neck, and he used that opportunity to turn around and whisper another spell. The wind picked up and sent Mr. Bain flying through the air.

"Ollie!" Levi was beside him. "Move out of the way. Now."

As his brother yanked him by the shoulder, Oliver felt the ground begin to shake.

Levi didn't even have to say anything for the huge chunks of earth to lift with his hands. They followed his silent command to shoot forward and crush themselves onto Mr. Bain's writhing body.

"Kara! Get Lynn over there!"

This was it. They were going to seal Mr. Bain's powers away, and he and his brother would finally be free. They'd finally be able to live without the constant fear of being preyed upon.

Lynn and Kara sprinted across the clearing.

If Lynn could do this, he'd forever be in her debt. Who knew that she, the only one out of the four of them without magic, would be the key to finally putting Oliver's mind at ease? This was proof that they were meant to be together…that they were supposed to meet that day. Fate brought them together in Massachusetts for a reason, he just didn't know what that reason was until now.

"No, no, no!"

Before Oliver could turn to ask his brother, the ground around Mr. Bain exploded, sending both Lynn and Kara's bodies flying. They hit the ground miles away with a loud thud.

"Lynn!" Oliver screamed, but neither of their bodies rose. "H-Hang on, I'm coming to-"

His feet wouldn't budge. He turned to his brother, who was also immobile.

"Oh, I know what you're doing." Eric laughed as he walked towards them. "Trying to be saints like your daddy, huh? Honestly, Levi, I expected a full out brawl."

Oliver couldn't even feel his fingers now as he tried to wiggle them. His shoulders, head, neck, arms, hips, and legs were all paralyzed. Even with Mr. Bain coming towards him, he couldn't muster up enough strength to shake.

"Stay away from him!" Levi yelled. "If you dare touch him-"

Oliver's breathing stopped when Mr. Bain's hand cupped his cheek. The cold metal that touched his neck was the next thing he felt, but he couldn't look down to see if there was really anything there.

"I was a fool to let you live for those three years," Mr. Bain whispered. "But the way you pleaded and screamed when I punished you was intoxicating. All the other workers on the boat were completely and totally obedient. But you – you still had that fight in your eyes that I couldn't take away. Now I know why."

"E-Even if you kill me, you won't get Levi," Oliver dared to say. "He's too powerful. More powerful than you'll ever be."

He could hear Levi yelling something, but he was too focused on the man before him. The kid from the woods who wanted to rip

Ollie apart. The young adult who was ready to kill his mother, father, and an infant Levi. The *evil* that fed on the fear, pain, and servitude of others.

"You think too highly of him," Mr. Bain said. "Your brother's just a scared little kid desperate for your approval. He's all talk, boy."

"Y-You're wrong."

"Yeah? He wasn't powerful enough to come save you off the ship, was he?" Mr. Bain smiled. "Or maybe he was. Maybe he was too scared or didn't care enough about you to risk his life."

"You're. Wrong."

The cold metal pressed harder against his neck, sending a sharp pain through his body and reassuring him that there really was something there.

"Then tell me why he didn't come and save you!" Eric said. "He was off having the time of his life around the world while you suffered!"

"Shut up!"

The ground below their feet started to heat up.

Oliver thought, as Mr. Bain looked down, that he would be surprised about the magic he was about to use. But when he glanced back up, his grin stretched from ear to ear, *mocking* him.

"Aw, your little hell fire spell isn't going to work on me, boy," he laughed. "I'm surprised you can even begin such powerful magic, but I bet you can't control-"

The ground split open and the fire, just as it did before, blew erratically from the fissure. This time, though, Levi wasn't there to stop it from continuing up into the sky and raining down.

The hold on Oliver that paralyzed every inch of his body released as another crack opened up directly between he and Mr. Bain. More fire spewed into the air, hitting Oliver and sending him rolling across the ground.

"L-Levi," Oliver whispered, barely able to hear his own voice. He could see his brother running to him.

Oliver raised up as much as he could, but for some reason his energy was sapping from his body faster than his mind had time to process.

"Shit! Ollie!" Levi said. "Y-Your neck!"

Oliver's eyes glazed over the burns on his arm as he touched his neck, and then brought his hand forward. The thin layer of red dripped into the grass, forming with the pool of blood already there.

"Dammit. Where the hell is Kara-"

Mr. Bain struggled to push himself from the ground miles away. The whole right side of his face was burned, as well as his clothes.

"You little shit."

Oliver watched the array of emotions on his brother's face. They changed so quickly he didn't have time to interpret them. But soon, Levi settled on one.

It reminded Oliver of the one he saw on his brother's face every time their father sent him away. The same one he had when he came back, expecting their parents – especially their mother – to welcome him home with open arms, but never did. It wasn't sad or defeated, it was accepting. It was like he thought that deep down this was what he deserved because he did something unforgivable.

Levi stood as Mr. Bain began limping his way towards them. Oliver tried to reach for him, but his arm was getting heavier by the second.

"Oliver," Levi said. "Stay here, okay? If you try to move, the bleeding will only get worse."

"W-Where are you-"

"I'll take care of this, yeah? Just stay here." Levi's voice was low and monotone. "And then we'll go get some ice cream, okay? You still like strawberry?"

Oliver nodded as he felt tears streaming down his face.

"I'll get you the biggest strawberry ice cream cone you've ever had, yeah? I promise."

With that, he walked forward, leaving Oliver alone on the cold, wet ground. He tried to grab for him again, but pain shot through his neck, and it became harder to breathe.

The sky darkened and rumbled with power. In the distance, Oliver could see lightning cut through the air like scissors through paper. His brother's fists were clenched as he stopped in front of Mr. Bain.

"L-Levi?" Oliver's voice gurgled.

Through squinted eyes, the scene in front of him looked like some kind of acrobatic light show. His brother's hand was illuminated with electrical energy, and Mr. Bain's with fire. But no matter how hard or how quickly they shot at one another, the other was fast enough to dodge. It reminded Oliver of their mother. They responded immediately to one another, like they knew one another *more than anyone else.*

But soon enough, Mr. Bain cried out. Oliver could see a spot on his shoulder smoking as he held it in pain. That didn't stop Levi, though. His brother took advantage of the moment by using the ground and rock below as projectiles.

"I used to be scared of you," he heard his brother say. "You used to keep me up at night. But now...now you don't have any power over me."

A loud clap of thunder sounded overhead, and the hair on Oliver's neck stood up.

He was almost getting too sleepy to watch, though. Even with his heart pounding, his body shivering from the cold, and his veins pumping with adrenaline, his eyes were getting heavy.

"Thunder!"

The bright streak of lightning was almost too much to look at as it hurled itself furiously from the clouds and into his brother's hand. Levi pulled his arm back the same way he used to when they played catch, and hurled the band over his shoulder.

Oliver braced himself against the ground as the impact of the blow engulfed him, trying its best to send him flying backwards. He could feel the electrical energy flowing through the ground, and he wasn't sure if it was the loss of blood, but Oliver could swear he could actually *see* it traveling in all different directions through the plains.

His eyes went back up, but the scene in front of him began to blur. He could still see his brother, but for some reason he was just standing there. His arm was twitching, and his hand was smoking but...there was something else. When Oliver squinted a little more, he could see the same black marks from Levi's hand on his neck and ear.

"Le..."

It took Mr. Bain a full minute before he could stand up, and when he did, Levi fell to his knees.

"You *rat.*" Mr. Bain choked out, blood running down his face. "I-I...don't care what kind of...*God* magic you use on me. You'll...*never* win."

"N-No." Oliver wrapped his hands around the grass in front of him and used it to pull himself forward. "Le...vi."

"Your grandfather couldn't...beat me," Mr. Bain said. "Y-Your mother couldn't beat me... and *you* can't...either."

Even as Oliver pulled himself forward, he was still so far away from his brother. Why wasn't Levi moving?

Mr. Bain picked Levi up by his throat, his other hand forming an icicle. His brother didn't even struggle, his body was loose and limp as his weight was supported in the air by Mr. Bain's arm.

"I…" Oliver struggled to keep moving forward. His body was getting lighter but pulling was getting harder. "F-F…"

"Come on, Ollie," Charlie said. "You said that's how you destroyed all the Lupus. Just do it again!"

"I can't figure it out," Oliver stared down at his hand. "I had to do it then. Or we would've died."

Charlie tapped her chin thoughtfully, completely oblivious to everything around her and lost in her own head.

He glanced nervously around. Now that they were on their own, it was his job to protect her. If he couldn't get this magic right, he'd fail her father.

"Then just think about what you did at the moment." Charlie grabbed his hand. "Reignite that power inside you. What were you thinking about?"

His hand wrapped around hers as he stared into the deep, soulful eyes before him.

"About how I have to protect the people I love," he said. "How I needed to protect you."

"Levi!"

Oliver's eyes came back into focus at the sound of Kara's voice. But it was so far away.

"Say…hello to Charlotte for me, rat."

His mother's voice echoed in his head as he saw Ollie fighting Mr. Bain with every bit of strength he had. He had to protect the people he loved. Levi, Lynn… he couldn't just lay over like this. Levi had been running and fighting this way his entire life, as had their mother. But here he was, after one blow, dragging his weak, barely conscious body across a clearing.

Dying.

Even though it burned, Oliver inhaled every bit of air he could and thrust his hand forward.

"Fire!"

As the beam of fire shot from his hand, he remembered the visions of his mother. How she shook with fear as she and *Ollie* ran through the forest and were cut off by an army of Lupus. Even though she was scared, she held her shoulders back as she blasted them with this same spell. He remembered her in the vision Mr. Bain had showed him earlier, too. How she fearlessly threw Macie behind her and took him on even though, again, her hands were shaking, and her skin was pale. She was so strong.

Levi was so strong.

But *Oliver*…

The string of fire shot through the back of Mr. Bain's chest, and he dropped Levi to the ground.

Why couldn't he be strong like them?

"Oliver!"

Mr. Bain fell to the ground, his body unmoving as it smoked.

"Levi!"

Why couldn't he protect the people he loved?

Why…did he feel so alone?

Chapter 11

"Oliver."

Oliver's eyes fluttered open as he sleepily scanned the luscious, full terrain around him. The grass his cheek lay on was bright green and soft like a pillow, and the sky...it was so clear and blue. Besides a few clouds, the only thing that obstructed his view were the tree leaves and their blood red flowers. He hadn't seen trees this beautiful since he was back home.

"Oliver?"

He felt like he'd been asleep for a long time. When he pulled himself into a sitting position, his whole upper body was almost too heavy.

He rubbed his eyes as the sun blinded him momentarily. When he blinked again, there was someone in front of him, but they were only a silhouette. The black figure was tall and curvy as it came towards him, with long hair and...were those tiny antlers?

"Who..." Oliver's voice trailed as the woman came into full view.

She had long, chestnut-colored hair that stretched a ways down her shoulders, over the top of her tawny-colored shoulders and-

"O-Oh!" He covered his eyes when he realized she was naked. "I'm sorry! I didn't know you were..."

"Hello, Oliver," the girl said. "Uncover your eyes. I'm not ashamed."

"W-Well, yeah, but you-" he peeked through his fingers. *"You're naked."*

Oliver felt warm hands wrap around his. Slowly they uncovered his eyes, revealing she was only inches away.

"Um," Oliver said. "Who are you?"

"I'm Cerva, Oliver," she said. Her finger poked his chest, the same place his mark was, and traced it through his shirt. "I'm the reason you have this."

Oliver's eyes went from his mark to the girl. This was the goddess of his mother's tribe? She didn't look like much of a goddess. She looked like she was the same age as Macie before she was killed.

"The curse of the prey?"

"That is…what your mother called it, yes." Cerva nodded. "It wasn't a curse before. It used to be an honor to bear the mark. But then the Lupus…"

"They attacked the village," Oliver said. "You were the one who showed me those visions of mom and Ollie?"

Cerva stood up and stared at the cloudless sky. The sunlight shined on her slightly wrinkled skin as she sighed loudly.

"No. When you were born, Ollie decided one life wasn't enough for him, so he became a part of you," she said. "When your mother sealed your mark, she unknowingly sealed him away, too. But then you started using your magic. The more you did, the more he was able to show you from his past."

"So, I'm Ollie?"

"Basically."

Oliver wrinkled his nose as he took that in.

He was a reincarnation of someone. That was something he wasn't expecting to learn. Then again, all of this tribal and magical stuff was just as far out there as reincarnation. That was just-

Oliver clutched his throat as the memories of what happened just moments ago flooded back to him.

They were in that field and...Levi was frozen, and Mr. Bain was about to kill him. He shot his fire through Mr. Bain's chest. But Oliver's neck was bleeding out so much he could hardly breathe. Did that mean he was...

"Where's Levi?" His head whipped from one direction to the other. "And Lynn and Kara? Why isn't my throat bleeding?"

"It's alright. Your brother's fine," she rolled her eyes. "Stupid kid was just reckless is all. I've told him time and time again not to put every single ounce of his energy into that thunder spell."

Oliver shook his head.

"What happened to him? Why wouldn't he move?"

"Well. Aside from nearly frying his brains out, parts of his nervous system shut down from all the electrical energy," Cerva said. "He knew that was a consequence, he just got overly ambitious. Per usual."

Cerva was talking about him like she knew him better than anyone else. He couldn't imagine his highly skeptical, unreligious brother talking to a goddess.

"I know what you're thinking. Levi's not the religious type," she grinned. "He actually is, though. Prays all the time. But he's still an asshole sometimes. No offense."

"No, he is," Oliver mumbled. "But he's...okay?"

Cerva nodded and offered her hand to help him up. He took it, surprised she had the strength.

"Yeah."

They walked through the thick, overgrown forest. Oliver thought it would be difficult, but the plants and roots seemed to part and make way for Cerva with each barefooted step. He looked behind them, noticing how much the path looked like a deer trail.

"And Mr. Bain?"

"Eric?" Cerva asked, and he nodded. "Oh, he's dead. You blew right through his filthy heart."

Those words sent a wave of relief through Oliver's body, which then instantly made him feel guilty. He knew this wasn't how his mother would've wanted it. She was peaceful and kind. Strong and patient.

"I can't believe I killed him."

"Why not? That man did horrible things," Cerva said. *"Not just to you and your brother, but the whole Cerva tribe. Your mother would be proud."*

"But I thought she didn't want to kill him?"

Cerva gave him a funny look.

"Your mother wanted to destroy him. It was your father who thought they could seal his powers away. It's possible, just stupid," she huffed. *"Your brother agreed with your plan because he thought you'd hate your mother. He didn't want that."*

They came to a large tree before they stopped. Cerva leaned up against it and slid to the ground. Oliver joined her, rubbing his hand through the smooth, damp dirt.

"So what now?"

"Hmm?"

"Now that Mr. Bain's gone, what now?"

Cerva shrugged her shoulders.

"I dunno. Spend time with Lynn or your brother," she said. *"It's over now. You're free."*

Oliver's eyebrows furrowed as he tilted his head at her.

"What? You think he's going to rise from the dead or something?" Cerva rolled her eyes. *"Only the Vulpes tribe can summon the dead. But they don't like Lupus too much. I wouldn't worry."*

Oliver stared down at his shoes as he thought about living a normal life. He'd never done that. How was he supposed to even know where to begin?

"Oh, and by the way, you're strong, too," Cerva said. "Just thought you should know."

"What?"

"Right before you passed out. You thought about how Levi and Charlotte were strong, but you didn't think you were," she said. "You're the one who killed Eric, you know."

He had no idea she could hear his thoughts. He wondered if she could hear them now.

"Levi would've been able to do it if I wasn't in the way. Or if he'd have gone at Mr. Bain with the intention to kill," Oliver said. "I made things harder."

"Wrong."

"Wrong?"

"Wrong." Cerva repeated. "Oliver, he would've been running the rest of his life. He's powerful because you make him that way."

Levi did mention that they'd been playing cat and mouse for a while. But just from watching him battle against Mr. Bain, Oliver could tell he was more than powerful enough to take him on at any point.

"Eric wasn't far off when he told you Levi's a scared little kid," she continued. "Levi's very scared, whether he wants to admit it

or not. But you gave him strength, Oliver. You had enough power over him to make him try to be a better person. That sounds pretty strong to me."

"Yeah..."

She smiled at him as he thought about that. But there was something that stuck in the back of his head that Mr. Bain had said. Was Levi's fear of Mr. Bain the reason he never came to save Oliver? Deep down, a part of him thought Levi was dead that whole time. Everyone else was.

Did he really give his brother the strength to finally take on their hunter?

The clouds above were beginning to darken and the wind picked up. When he looked to Cerva, her eyes were narrowed as she stared up into the endless sky.

"Alright. Time for you to go."

Cerva stood, once again offering her hand to help him up.

"Will I see you again?" Oliver asked.

"Maybe. Levi visits me often. It'd be nice to get a break from only seeing him all the time."

Cerva reached out, her finger tracing his mark through his shirt.

"Goodbye, Oliver. Good job."

"Good-"

"Oliver?"

He covered his face as bright lights invaded his vision. But this time they were artificial ones from a ceiling, not the sun.

"Oh my god! Oliver!"

Blue hair clouded his line of sight as he was pulled into a tight but also painful hug. His throat hurt as he coughed from the pressure of Lynn's shoulder on it. The aching was excruciating.

"L-Lynn?" Oliver asked, and she pulled away. "Hey."

"Hey," she whispered, her autumn eyes warming his cold body. "Y-You're okay."

Oliver looked around the room. He had no idea where they were at. There were beeping sounds, a strong disinfectant smell, and machines hooked to tubes going to his arm, which went to-

"What the?" His eyes zeroed in on the needles. "Why are these – what are these?"

"No, no!" Lynn grabbed his hands before they could yank the needles out. "They're giving you important fluids through those."

The beeping on the machine accelerated as Oliver's heart jumped. Where were they, and what were all these crazy things?

"Wait a minute," Oliver said. "Lynn, you're dad. Where's your dad?"

Lynn's eyes went dark instantly. They were a night and day difference as she played with her short, untrimmed hair.

"He's…gone, Oliver," she said. "Levi told me they found out where Mr. Bain was rooming at and my dad was there. He killed him."

"L-Lynn, I'm sorry." His hand wrapped around hers. "I really am."

"It's not your fault."

Oliver pushed himself from the bed so he was sitting in a more comfortable position. Breathing was still hard regardless of how he sat, though.

"No, it is my fault. If I wouldn't have…" He shook his head. "Maybe if I didn't make you come to New York, he'd still be-"

"I'm glad I came with you to New York, Oliver," Lynn said. "I was sick. A mess. Being in that hotel just dug me into a deeper hole each day I woke up. You saved me."

He saved her. That's what he felt like she did for him. If she hadn't stopped him from going after the ship, he would've drowned. Or Mr. Bain would've killed him if he was able to catch up to them. And all the times she pushed him to be better. *She* was the one who saved *him*.

Lynn's hand pressed against his cheek.

"I love you, Oliver."

"Oh! Um, well," Oliver felt his cheeks redden. "I…I love you too, Lynn. I think I have for a long time."

She leaned forward again, hugging him as tightly as she could. It still hurt, but he'd have time to rest later. Right now, this was exactly what he needed.

"Gross." Levi pulled the curtain out of the way as he walked in. "Get a room."

"Mr. Lee, the doctor hasn't cleared you to even be out of bed yet. You really need to-"

Levi glared at the nurse, and she turned without another word and walked away. He winced ever so slightly, but it didn't wipe the playful grin from his face.

"Levi, stop doing that to the poor nurse," Kara growled. "She's just doing her job."

"I don't need anymore treatment. You patched me all up," he said. "How are you, Ollie? You feeling okay? Lynn?"

Oliver's eyes locked on his brother's right hand – the one he threw the thunder with. It was twitching drastically every five seconds.

"I think Kara healed all my cuts and bruises," Lynn said. "I've never been flung that far or hard before. It was crazy."

It twitched again, even when he wasn't moving it or doing anything else.

"Yeah, you guys flew pretty far," Levi said, his eyes falling on Oliver. "What is it, buddy?"

"Y-Your hand," Oliver said. "Why's it doing that?"

Levi rolled his eyes and made a 'pshhh' sound.

"Ah, it's nothing, yeah? Just a little-"

"I couldn't heal him entirely," Kara said. "With the irreversible damage the thunder did to his nervous system, he's going to have that twitch forever."

"Battle scar," Levi corrected her. "Not a big deal at all."

Oliver watched Levi laugh as Kara punched his arm. His brother was happy, something he wasn't used to seeing ever. It was nice-

"This is breaking news!" the TV above them said. "Upcoming magician Oliver Lee has been found and is recovering in the Elizabeth Conway University Hospital behind me. No one has been able to get into his room to interview him yet."

"Oh," Oliver said. "People know where I'm at now."

"I had to call an ambulance," Kara said. "I could heal your throat, but I couldn't replenish the blood you lost. It was too much."

Oliver could faintly remember it now. It hurt so bad, and he was sure his lungs had filled up with blood almost entirely at one point. At least that was what it felt like. And he had no idea how he was able to muster up the strength at the end to use that fire spell.

There was a knock at the door.

"Oliver? Oliver, I hope you're decent because I'm coming in," Nik's voice called from the other side of the door. "Hey! Look who it is!"

Nik's ragged face smiled big as he stepped inside.

"Hey Nik," Oliver said.

"Hey Nik? That's all you have to say?" Nik laughed. "Dude, what happened to you? And who are these two?"

"That's my brother and his girlfriend."

Both Levi's and Kara's faces reddened at the word girlfriend.

"Well, uh, yeah. Girlfriend." Levi scratched the back of his head. "Name's Levi, and this is Kara."

"I've heard a lot about you, Levi!" Nik said, shaking Levi's hand. "I'm-"

"You're Nik Rafiel, of course," Levi interrupted. "I actually saw your show when you came to Russia the last time."

Nik turned to Oliver and ruffled his hair.

"See, kid? Again, that's the reaction I expect," he said. "Anyway, I told the reporters outside you were kidnapped, your brother came to save you, and he killed the kidnapper. Done. I don't know what actually happened, but…"

"That's basically the gist of it," Oliver mumbled. "Thanks, Nik."

"Well, you know how those reporters are," he said. "Scary little guys and girls. They can twist around what you say in seconds and before you know it, *you're* the bad guy. Sheesh."

Oliver sighed in relief as everyone continued to talk and laugh together. Lynn kept a firm hold of his hand, rubbing it with her thumb every once in a while.

Cerva was right. Everything *was* okay now. He and his brother could go on and live normal lives now without worrying about getting hunted. The mark on his chest and on Levi's back were no longer a *curse of the prey*, but a symbol of how even with the odds stacked against someone, there was still hope.

He and his brother, against all odds, had survived.

Epilogue

Levi sighed as he let the warm air hit his face outside the hospital. All those needles and blood…it was all way too much.

As he pulled a cigarette from his pocket, his hand twitched, nearly sending it flying across the parking lot. It caught him off guard at first, because he still wasn't used to it, but he guessed he'd better be fast. He was surprised that his hand having a permanent twitch was the only permanent consequence he'd suffered.

He knew the consequences of putting all his magic and energy into his thunder spell; he just hadn't expected it to be so drastic. The electricity felt like it took *hours* to travel through his body and do the damage it did. Everything had been in slow motion, and he couldn't breathe, feel anything, or even think. Even Eric picking him up was slow. The first time he experienced sensation again was when Oliver's fire magic went through Eric's chest. He could feel the heat from it as it barely missed him.

Levi stuck the cigarette in his mouth and crossed his eyes so he could see the end of it. It instantly ignited, and he inhaled its deep, relaxing panacea.

He knew after all this time that he should be thankful and jumping with joy. Eric was finally dead, his family was at peace, and he could relax for a while…but…

"Levi?" Kara said. "Hey, you're smoking? You haven't done that since Russia. What's the matter?"

As he exhaled, he stared down at the stick in his hand. It looked the same as the ones from Russia, but they tasted different.

"Something's not right."

"What?"

"Something…" Levi had no idea what he was trying to say. "I have a bad feeling, Kara."

She sat on the stairs beside him and sighed.

"About what?"

"I don't know," Levi said. "It's just this feeling of impending doom."

Maybe it was because the norm for him was constant chaos. He'd gotten so used to it that he felt weird without it. Or it could've been because the last time he'd come to America, things had gotten ugly, and now that his body didn't have to worry about Eric anymore, it was finding other things.

"I think you just worry too much," Kara said. "Come on. Oliver's been asking about where you went."

This was definitely nothing he'd felt before. He couldn't even explain it to the voice in his head, which was shrugging its imaginary shoulders and rolling its eyes at him.

He *did* worry a lot. This had to be nothing more than a fluke in his thinking. Maybe the thunder did that, too.

"Levi?"

"I'm coming."

He flicked the cigarette to the ground as he took one last look at the busy city before him.

He was just imagining things. Eric was dead. There was nothing for him to brood over anymore, but he knew he'd probably feel even better once they got out of America.

A smile returned to his face as he thought about Oliver. After all these years, they were finally together, with nothing to fear.

Things couldn't get any better than this.

Megan Ransdell is a wielder of magic and darkness. She builds worlds only to tear them down piece by piece, mountain by mountain, all for the enjoyment of –

Okay, she's actually an author, but what's the difference?

Megan enjoys writing fantasy and has an especially soft spot for creating magic heavy worlds. In order to keep her magic powers a secret, she has cleverly disguised herself as a college student working towards her B.S. in Psychology.

Now You See Me, her debut novella, released in February 2019. *Now You Don't* is her second novella to hit the shelves, but she's far from done.

Megan also writes for the magazine *Envie! A Magazine for the Literary Curious* as a mental health writer.

Made in the USA
Middletown, DE
12 November 2019

78380232R00094